ELIZABE[...]

C000071495

RING
AROUND
THE
LUNA

ILLUSTRATIONS BY
MILLICENT HODSON

RING AROUND THE LUNA

This is a work of fiction. Resemblances to historical persons are intentional and imagined.

Typeset in Book Antiqua and Carnivalee Freakshow by Chris Hansen.

ISBN 978-0-9892521-4-0

Black & white paperback edition, first published independently by Trapeze Press and printed by CreateSpace. For full-color edition, visit author website.

To My Mermother

Welcome to Coney Island,

Buff
Graduate of the Incubator Baby House;
a natural-born story-teller

Paloma Bright
Buff's sidekick since the cradle;
raised on Luna's light

Doctor Martin Couney
Impresario of the Incubator Babies;
life-saver and showman

Handsome Henry
Barker of the Seaside Circus Sideshow;
soft-hearted carny

Myrtle Crespi
Crowned the Mermaid Queen,
no stranger to danger

The Commissioner
Builder of the World's Fair &
Sworn foe of Coney Island

Chief Ramsey
Bamboozled top cop of the boardwalk

Mingus Lamont
Shifty manager of Steeplechase Park

The World's Favorite Playground!

Captain Clyde
Skipper of The Mickey;
navigator of Coney Island Creek

Nurse Breddy
Head honcho of the Incubator Baby House;
able to see Couney's kiss at first blush

Madame Fortuna
a.k.a Rita Chervinsky;
fortune teller with a debt and a conscience

The Flame-Eating Totem
Tattooed fire-eater of the Sideshow;
a gal named Angelica

The Funny Face Gang
Jinx, Bugs, Snake and Lou;
bad apples, all

&

The Mermother
Safeguarding Coney Island
from her underwater watchtower

Full Moon
June 20, 1939

*S*ome nights the moon over Coney Island mirrors the electric glow of the famous amusement park with a wide, luminous smile. Some nights it winks, a crescent reflection of boardwalk pranks. But other nights, it peers over the beach bungalows like the bloodshot eye of a Cyclops.

This night is such a night.

On this night, when America tosses and turns and worries about jobs and money and unfair fights, the spirit of Coney Island wanes thin under a full moon. The majestic Wonder Wheel grinds to a halt in the thick haze, and the brass bands on the Bowery fall mute in the fug. In the unsettled hush, the Mermother rises from her underwater den and fingers the air – touching, testing.

For all these years of Great Depression, her presence in the surf has been enough to keep merriment alive on land. But tonight the shore is stalked by a shadow. The cloud that covers the beach is too dark. People have begun to take cover, and Coney Island can't survive when folks seek shelter over sunshine.

In the long water off Brooklyn's southern tier, the Mermother feels anxiety like a cold spring rising. She watches the moon quiver and slip behind midnight gloom, full of unborn light.

CHAPTER ONE

It's not yet nine o'clock, and the sun has come and gone. Just a brief appearance over the Rockaways and then it retreated behind the same gray haze that has bullied its way into every summer day since the season began.

Standing knee-high in the surf, Buff shivers. He isn't cold, not exactly. Chilled, maybe. But not by the sunless sky. And not by the ocean, which is a respectable bathing temperature for a late June morning.

The boy fixes his eyes on his goal, which rocks two hundred yards from shore: a wide floating platform, slick with sea-slime and spiked with barnacles. In its center hangs a tarnished fisherman's bell. The buoy-bell bobs but makes no sound in waves too gentle to ring its iron clangor.

Buff wades further into the surf, rising on his toes as the water reaches his skinny thighs. He swings his arms in front of his chest – one, two, three – like the wrestlers at the Pike before they launch a knockout body slam. With a gasp he flings himself forward into a graceless belly flop. He dips his face into the water and strikes out for the bell.

Eyes shut tight, legs kicky-splashy, Buff swims his odd version of a crawl. Pushing aside thoughts of what lies below, the boy imagines himself atop the floating platform, waving to a cheering crowd on the beach. He imagines the water littered with carnations, like the stage at the end of the opera Doc took him to that one time.

In his head, Buff hears the heroic anthem of warrior Vikings as they ply the stormy waves.

Glory be, glory be, I'm the prince of the sea.

"Flat," whispers Buff to the melody.

The vision vanishes. The tune dies. Buff breaks his stroke and lifts his head. The buoy is still far. Very far. Buff turns to look back at the shore. Also far. But not as far as the buoy. He treads water, feeling the hateful tingle in his legs – the one that always gets the better of him.

Buff is not a strong swimmer. It isn't that he's physically weak or especially uncoordinated, though, to be sure, he is still a bit of a runt at age thirteen. The problem is that he hasn't gotten the hang of letting his body take over for his mind. Instead of pushing his arms and legs forward toward the bell, he lets his brain tread hypothetical circles:

Can I swim more? How much more?

Just far enough to be too far to swim back?

Buff considers that point - too far but not far enough. And the more Buff thinks, the less he swims, and so, as always, he flounders between here and there. Finally, he tucks his face back into the water and takes several more strokes, trying to ignore the numb weight of his feet.

Why do they do that?

I use them every day. Walk the boardwalk all day long.

Why should this be any different?

Feet out there flopping like fish in a bucket.

Buff jerks upright, startled by a light sensation across his leg. He looks into the water below but he can see nothing beyond its dull surface. He doesn't like not knowing what was down there. Hates it more than not being able to swim so good. He hates, too, the cold current that is creeping around his ankle.

Buff turns and swims back to shore. In his mind he sees the crowd on the beach trudging back to the boardwalk. In his ears he hears only the pumping of his disappointed heart. He recognizes the rhythm.

"The blues," whispers Buff.

Back on the beach the boy grabs his towel and spits salt into the sand. He clamps his toes into its firm dampness and feels safe.

It's strange, he thinks eyeing the white track of scum left by the tide, *how that line divides life and death. But it's always shifting.*

He is thinking of the turtles, of course – the flippered babies scampering madly for the sea while all of nature tries to stop them. Buff has good reason to identify with them – he, too, faced death the moment he was born. He survived. But since then, he's never really been tested. That's what he realized last month, when he was digging with Paloma for periwinkles under the pier and instead they found a baby sea-turtle. It lay white-belly up, with no sign of whatever had stopped it from reaching the sea. Buff can remember what it felt like in his hand: light, but not empty. Dead, all right, but with something still alive inside, pushing tiny bubbles from translucent membranes. He remembers the small pool of water left in his palm when he put the turtle back on the sand. The tide must have reached the creature after all … once it was too late.

That was the day Buff decided he would swim in solidarity with the sea turtles.

If a minute-old baby can run a quarter mile to the sea, I can swim to the dang bell.

He gave himself till the end of the season to do it.

I got time, he thinks now, watching the rocking platform. *Two more months of summer.*

But he's not so sure. He can't say why, but today Buff feels that time has gotten shorter, and that - overnight even - reaching the buoy and ringing the bell have become more important than anything ever has been or ever will be. He's surprised by the urgency. It's strong – stronger, maybe, than Buff's resolve; certainly stronger than his wobbly legs.

7

Buff turns his back on the sea. Ahead of him stretches the Coney Island skyline. A wooden range of roller coasters, each scaled by a man with a hammer. All along the boardwalk comes the sound of metal on metal: the trackmen testing the bolts.

It is, like everything on Coney, music to Buff's ears. In the valleys between those manmade peaks of the coasters the carnies are opening their food and game stalls. Buff hears the muffled song of the carousel as it winds up to speed. He smells the popcorn pans expel yesterday's butter. He sees the great Wonder Wheel float like a mirage in the thick haze of the morning.

It plays tricks on your eyes, the Wonder Wheel does. Seems to turn sometimes in the dead of night. Appears to stand still in the middle of the day. This morning Buff thinks he sees a glimmering halo, like someone developed a giant double exposure of the Ferris wheel in last night's humid darkroom.

Not that you should expect anything at Coney to look right any more, thinks Buff. *The weather being what it is. Not really weather in fact.More like a bad mood that rode in on a cloud.*

Buff thinks of the picture of Apollo in his much-thumbed book of Greek Gods. Apollo rode a chariot, dragged the sun around with him.

If we were still in ancient days, thinks Buff, *we'd blame the gods for carrying off the Coney Island sunshine.*

And the crowds.

And the fireworks.

And the shrieks of laughter.

And the children.

Especially the children.

Buff turns his gaze to the Funny Face, the enormous billboard of light bulbs that sits atop Steeplechase Park. The Funny Face flashes too many teeth in its grin - an advertisement for the hilarity inside the Pavilion of Fun.

Even the Funny Face feels it, Buff thinks, eyeing the manic mascot.

It – whatever it is that is pressing down on the boardwalk, elbowing out the sun, exhausting the mechanical rides. Whatever it is that has sucked the hysterical out of the old Funny Face and replaced it with hysteria.

Used to be, kids pointed at the Face and laughed. Now, they hide behind their mother's skirts.

I don't blame them, Buff thinks.

Crazy-lookin' face is downright alarming. Especially when you consider what's been happening this season.

The Funny Face has a catchphrase.

"Looka, Looka, Looka!" he's supposed to be saying.

Ask me, thinks Buff, he's saying *Watch Out*.

9

CHAPTER TWO

A whistle – a long low note followed by two short shots: Henry. Buff smiles and runs the rest of the way to the boardwalk, where a man with a marvelous mustache sits on a weathered bench.

"I thought we had a deal that you wouldn't go swimming without me."

The man called Handsome Henry acts younger than his age but he feels older than his years. Buff reminds Henry of a day when things were different, and he had plenty of time to grow up. He leans forward and pulls a piece of kelp from the boy's sagging swimsuit. He says, "You know what can happen even to strong swimmers in a bad undertow."

"That undertow is about as strong as I am," says Buff. "Fair fight, I guess."

The man pauses, weighing his words as carefully as those he uses every day on the bally stage to lure an audience from the street to the ticket office and into the darkened mystery of the Sideshow tent. Handsome Henry, the bally-man, knows that timidity is often just a shadow of a too-bright bravery. "Even if you did make it all the way to the buoy, it would be a shame if there wasn't nobody around to see it," he concludes.

Buff wraps his towel around his head like a swash-buckler and hops up onto the planked boardwalk. He is an unusual-looking boy. He wears his hair so long it curls over his ears. A handful of freckles splashes across his wide face like a shy constellation. He looks nothing like Henry, or like the little brother Henry still mourns. But Henry feels closer to the boy than to the shoes on his wandering feet. He smiles under his walrus whiskers and follows Buff's gaze out to the end of the skeleton Dream-land Pier, to the buoy bell.

"You'll get there, Buff."

Buff nods. "Sure I will."

A gull swoops low over the boardwalk benches and squawks. The sweet smell of candy apples wafts in from the Bowery. There's a giggle from under the planks. "Hiya, Handsome. Hello, Buff."

"Morning, Myrtle," says Henry, tipping his hat to the redhead peeking above the edge of the boardwalk. "You're out and about early today."

"Fact is - I never went in," answers the young woman. "Didn't you hear I was crowned Mermaid Queen? I had to celebrate, dontcha know. And, of course, thank all my supporters and entertain all my whattayacall it..."

Henry and Buff wait.

"Constituents," she finishes and wipes sand from her knees.

Myrtle Crespi's long red hair is unbrushed and wild. There appear to be seashells in it. Myrtle keeps a bungalow down in Sheepshead Bay that she says is neat as a pin, but her spectacular appearance suggests a life of natural disorder. Buff, who has known her as long as he's known the boardwalk, sees Myrtle as a perfect complement to Henry – peers not just in age but in vanity, too. He suspects she spends as much of her morning teasing her Medusa tresses as Henry gives his glistening hair pomade.

"Where's your crown then, Miss Myrtle?" Henry asks.

"Oh boys, it was a heckuva of a contest," she replies. "First they couldn't decide between Lola Fincastle and Betty from Brighton. I had to step in and demonstrate how neither of them was worthy of being Queen. Goodness, how everyone laughed when I showed up with my bucket of jellyfish! I'll betcha Betty's still shrieking."

"Doesn't sound too lady-like," says Henry, extending a hand to help her onto the boardwalk.

"No place for ladies. It's the Mermaid Queen Pageant," Myrtle replies. "I just wish I hadn't used my lovely green cape to hog-tie that judge. He actually took his penknife to it. Didn't accept my apology and then refused to say he was sorry for shredding my costume. Lost an awful lot of shimmer-scales demonstrating my flying fish technique on the bar, too," Myrtle adds ruefully, squeezing her backside in between Henry and Buff.

"Now wasn't that lucky for the bar?" says the bally-man.

Buff listens absent-mindedly to the familiar banter. He knows the tune well. It is playful, promising. You could almost sing along – but that would be teasing, and Buff doesn't tease his friends.

"Don't pageants have some kinda talent act?" Handsome Henry is asking.

"Sure. I played "Three Little Fishies" on the washboard."

"A virtuoso performance, no doubt."

"Honest to gosh, Handsome, if only that young squib from the radio hadn't drunk too much rum, I'd be booked on variety shows all across the country tonight."

Myrtle clears her throat and warbles: "Three little fishies, but not enough to eat…"

Her song is interrupted by the call of a newsboy.

"Read all about it! Morning edition! Another kid gone missing from Coney Island boardwalk! Read all about it! Fourth disappearance this summer! Cops beat! Read it! Read it!"

CHAPTER THREE

Henry is up like a shot. He returns to the bench, reading in snatches from the paper: "An eight-year-old girl, blonde braids, last seen by the pony ride across from the Wonder Wheel... Mother and father held for questioning... Police Officer Sherman Ramsey requesting assistance... No further developments in the cases of the three other children reported missing while visiting Coney Island earlier this month..."

Henry lifts his bowler hat and rubs his forehead. "Darndest thing," he finally says. "Little girls don't just wander off. Those boys what got lost before, maybe. But not a little girl. Little girl goes missing, you got yourself a kidnapper. And how's a kidnapper gonna grab a kid from the middle of the park without anybody seeing?"

Buff watches Henry, a man who counts himself among the keenest-eyed carnies on Coney Island. Here's a fella spends his days scanning the crowds on Cantilever Walk and nights counting cards at the Faro table behind Lorenzo's clam bar.

"I've been known to see a fight before it happens and

a heart the moment it breaks." That's what Handsome Henry boasts on the outdoor bally stage of the Seashore Circus Sideshow fifteen times a day.

But most folks, thinks Buff, *even the ones with two good eyes, have a hard enough time seeing what's happening right in front of them.*

That's especially true on Coney Island. Folks come looking for smoke and mirrors down at Coney.

Expect the unexpected.

Prepare to be dazzled.

You won't believe your eyes.

That's what we've always sold at Coney Island, he thinks. And now children are vanishing. In full daylight. Without a trace. There's really no choice down here these days but to believe what your eyes can't see.

Buff feels a tingling, like when his feet went queer in the water. Only now it isn't his feet, it is in his chest.

"Dollars to donuts somebody saw," he says.

Henry looks at the boy, cocks an eyebrow.

"Paper says no witnesses."

But Buff knows something that Henry doesn't. He knows that when each of the three children went missing, Officer Ramsey had a handful of people stop into the precinct all foggy and confused. Said they had seen something, but couldn't say what. Wanted to report something lost, but couldn't remember what.

"Boardwalk bamboozlement," Officer Ramsey calls it. But Buff suspects something stronger than twenty-cent hard cider. His legs tremble slightly, remembering the pull of the buoy-bell and the tug of the tide.

Something natural.

Something elemental.

Something unstoppable, like the waning moon.

It is awful, though – four disappearances in just two weeks; children vanishing in the funparks; mothers and fathers blinking in confusion; and still they bring them down to the beach. It's as if parents, worn out by the long decade of Depression, have given up. Better to trust in some benevolent God of Coney to look after their kids.

Buff thinks of his own guardian – a doting old man who surely loves him, but who considered his job done the day Buff learned to walk, talk and feed himself satisfactorily. Doc, after all, had saved Buff's infant life by keeping him under close observation. Now, it seemed that he had decided that was the best way to see the boy through childhood as well – by keeping an eye on him, no more and no less. It was a well-intentioned sort of observation, relaxed a bit more every year and supplemented with humor and chocolate Ovaltine.

"I've got my eye on you!" Doc would shout every morning as Buff left for school, even if his aging eyes were taking a catnap under his winking spectacles.

That's when they disappear, Buff thinks, *when they stop being seen.*

"They give a name?" he asks now.

"Mary Lou Walker, it says."

Myrtle sighs. "Poor little mites. Didn't anyone ever teach 'em to scratch a fella's eyes out?" She stands, straightens her skirt and pats her wild hair. "Well, all I can say is, tragedy makes me hungry. How about breakfast, Handsome?"

"I could eat," Henry says. "Buff? Hungry?"

"Nah," says the boy. He squints up at the heavy sky, streaked with an indeterminate daylight. "Think I'll stay a bit before I open up the booth, dry off in this piddly sun."

"Okay, sport," says Henry, placing his hat on his head. "I'll see you here tomorrow? Before you go swimming?"

"Sure," says Buff. He accepts a light squeeze on his shoulder from Henry's long fingers and winks at Myrtle, who hoots in response. Then he watches them amble down the boardwalk – Myrtle all arms and hips; Henry a slim silhouette, dark on gray.

See you here tomorrow – that's what Henry had said. *See you here.* Buff thinks they are the words of a man who knows to keep watching.

Down at the water a lone heron slaps its great wings. It dives and, with a splash, plucks its breakfast from the waves. There is a moment's glint as the bird tosses the fish into the morning air and catches it squarely in its gullet.

Mother Nature's own disappearing act, thinks Buff.

He rises to go.

As he stands, he notices something lying under the bench. He bends down and picks up a rag doll with button eyes and yarn hair, her sprawling arms akimbo and her skirt fluttering in the breeze.

Something in Buff's head shifts just then, like the sound of a carousel calliope as it cranks up for the first ride of the day. An image of a young girl's anxious face flashes in his mind. It is turned upwards as if to answer a question: *Whaddya do that for?*

The calliope in his head picks up speed, and a slide-show of images whizzes through the Buff's muddled mind: clasped hands; tight lips; an orb, soft and melting; a broken spire, a single teardrop. They are moving too fast now, in time with a gathering melody that grows clearer even as it becomes sinister: *We all fall down, we all fall down.*

Buff covers his ears and sees again the double rings of the Wonder Wheel, sees the cars sliding on their tracks. And again — the girl's face, bereft and pale, framed by the great Ferris wheel. *Mother?* she asks … and then a sudden upward draft leaves emptiness, like a newspaper expelled from the subway tracks by an approaching train.

"Oh," says Buff, blinking sweat from his eyes, "I saw it happen."

CHAPTER FOUR

Buff walks down Surf Avenue lost in thought. *I wasn't even near the Wonder Wheel yesterday. Or was I? How near do you need to be to see something you aren't watching?*

On Coney Island, it is easy to be in two places at once. Because if you aren't there now, you probably either ust were or are about to be.

This summer is so rutted in mid-season malaise, it's hard to tell one day from another: Breakfast, boardwalk, story-booth and back. With detours, always, of course.

Did I stop off on Jones Walk for a game of skin-the-wire?

Or take a cruise on the creek with Clyde?

Was it yesterday I shot a round of water balloons with Paloma before dinner?

Buff wiggles a finger in his ear, fishing for the tune.

Was the girl Mary Lou listening to my stories in the booth?

Buff pictures the snug stall with its freshly painted sign: TALL TALES FROM A SHORT KID : SESSIONS DAILY FOR ALL AGES... When he hung that sign at the beginning of the season, it seemed like a swell idea. Buff, after all, was a "natural born story-teller." That's what everybody on Coney Island had told him for years. So when he posted his daily schedule of Stories from Exotic Destinations & Tales of Magic plus Death Defying Rescues & Amazing Legends of Luna Park Lore... Buff imagined hordes of rapt youngsters tugging at their folks' hands, pointing and pleading to visit the story-teller.

But the booth, like all of Coney Island, has been unnaturally quiet for weeks. Yesterday was no different.

The tune winds its way like a worm.

We all fall down. We all fall down.

Buff reaches Surf Avenue. He looks east and west - Coney Island's main drag is as empty as a desert. He walks the long blocks past closed souvenir shops and stops at the entrance to Luna Park - once a grand portal to an electric, eclectic funpark, now just an extra-wide metal roll-down gate topped by faded whirligigs that no longer whirl.

A girl in dungaree overalls steps out of a small door cut into the gate, followed by a parade of cats. She sees Buff and scowls in mock disapproval.

"Late again, story-boy? You got a whole mess of kiddos at your booth wriggling like worms in a bait box. 'Open up!' They're shouting."

Buff smirks. "Fat chance."

The girl pulls a bundle wrapped in a greasy napkin from her pocket. The cats hurl themselves at her legs in a mewling melee. She kicks lightly, tisks loudly, and corrals the cats into the alley, high-dangling the carcass of a fish.

Buff has to yell to be heard over the cat clamor: "Hey Paloma - were we at the Wonder Wheel yesterday?"

"Think we might have – HEY watch it, that's my finger, you minx! Didn't we fill up Angelica's kerosene jug from the machine room? Or was that the day before - OH NO YOU DON'T, YOU FAT BULLY!"

Paloma emerges from the alley in a puff of feline fur. "I shoulda known better than to let that one-eyed tiger come for breakfast. He's a real bully. Ran off with the whole head!"

She stuffs the dirty napkin into one pocket and pulls a heavy ring of keys from another. "Guess you're asking because you heard the news already?"

But Buff doesn't answer. He's humming the tune again, his eyes fixed on the faded whirly-gigs of Luna Park. Words tease like spirals.

Ring around the luna... pocket full of tuna....

Paloma shrugs. "Dreamer," she mutters. She unlocks the four padlocks on the gate and Buff follows her, his friend since infancy, into the Park that he knows like the back of his hand.

Thousands of lucky boys and girls call Coney Island home. It's a place where families and back gardens grow up alongside circus tents and coo-chee dancers. But Buff and Paloma's connection to Coney is even more precious than the bonds of childhood. They are among those who owe their lives to one particular pavilion located in a far corner of the world-famous playground called Luna Park. It's a whitewashed building with a frieze on its façade of babies' rattles and tiny cupids. It's where folks drop their nickels in the turnstiles to see the impossibly small creatures nested inside – the Incubator Babies.

Buff and Paloma were two such babies. They weighed six pounds at birth – if you put them on the scales together. That happened daily inside the Incubator Baby House, where they lay side by side in special cribs fitted with an ingenious growlamp. Born too early, they would have never survived if left to modern medicine. Born lucky, they instead found their way to a place where their premature entry was treated as a curiosity rather than a death sentence.

The Impresario of the Incubator Baby House was Doctor Martin Couney, a man who brought New Ideas from the Old World. But when Doc Couney presented his Human Incubator technology to the doctors in New York, they sneered. They took one look at the glowing glass breadbox and called it a "child hatchery." Couney, they said, was a quack. So the good doctor turned on his back on the men with

22

their degrees and considered the rest of America, with its penchant for gambling. He saw a nation that favored underdogs, hobbled horses and fixed fights. *So why wouldn't they bet on a baby with slim odds?* he figured. That's when Doc Couney took his incubators to where people paid money to see something you didn't see everyday.

"It takes a lot of pennies to keep the lights on," he said, slapping down his first summer's rent for the small pavilion on the outer perimeter of Luna Park.

Since then, hundreds of babies, some almost too tiny to see, have found their way to the Incubator Baby House. Sometimes they are brought by Doc himself – like the one who was supposed to be born on Valentine's Day but was delivered, instead, in St. Mary's Hospital in Buffalo, New York while the new year of 1926 was still brand new. The baby didn't cry at all, though his mother made enough noise for the both of them. In fact, she didn't stop hollering until the doctors had examined the infant and written on the chart, with a sad shake of the head, NOT VIABLE. By then, the mother had left St Mary's without her silent scrap of an infant. It happened that Doctor Martin Couney was also in Buffalo that cold winter night.

"Nonsense," he said with his Old World certainty when he read the chart above the bassinet. He lifted the abandoned infant from its scratchy blanket and it squawked at the frosty air. "Eureka," said Doc Couney, and he hurried back to Luna Park, where he deposited Baby Buffalo Doe, "Buff," into an incubator alongside the baby girl born the night before to a Bowery dancer called Louisa Bright.

In the thirteen years since, Paloma has sprouted a set of long, strong legs, while Buff has remained a puny promise of a man. People who know where they came from sometimes tease that Paloma must have stolen Buff's light bulbs at night.

"That's women for you," Buff likes to reply to salty laughter.

Coney Island is a place that attracts people with a streak of strange, just as surely as a magnet pulls a pin. But for Doc Couney's Incubator Babies, resident miracles of science and showbiz, that streak is more like an umbilical cord. More than anyone else on Coney Island, Buff and Paloma are in tune with the place's life-giving power. Which is why they feel, more acutely than most, the daily tug in June 1939 that is the warmth and light draining from their home.

CHAPTER FIVE

In Luna Park's central plaza, Officer Sherman Ramsey is pacing. "Four missing persons cases," he grumbles. "You'd think it would be enough for headquarters to send in a squad of detectives wouldn't ya? But, no – I can't get one lousy extra lieutenant for backup. And you know why?" The policeman jabs a finger at Lionel Bangs, the manager of Luna Park. Lionel does know why, but he turns off his hose and lets Ramsey tell him again.

"I'll tell you why. Because the Parks Commissioner has ordered every square foot of his precious World's Fair has gotta have a cop on beat. Oh yeah, there's no shortage of Blue over in Flushing today. A kid couldn't go missing at the Fair long enough to stop up a drinking fountain with chewing gum – not without the Commissioner himself heading up the All Points Bulletin."

Officer Ramsey mutters one last protest under his breath and angrily kicks a stone from under his tired leather boot. Buff watches it skitter across the square. He's heard it before, the trash talk aimed at the Commissioner and his World's Fair. The Fair opened up about a month ago, twenty miles north in Flushing, Queens, and still it was all you heard on the radio, on the subway, and anywhere north of Coney Island, which hunkered down on Brooklyn's bottom, feeling like the butt of a joke.

Buff feels sorry for them – the carnies and showmen who thought good times couldn't be had two places at once. Sure, he has no love for the Commissioner. How could he defend a guy who had declared Coney Island a public nuisance? But Buff is a thirteen-year-old boy who has rarely left Brooklyn. He is terribly, if secretly, curious to see what the fuss up in Flushing is all about – good or bad.

"Seems like everybody's looking for a reason to spend time at the Fair," he says. "I figure every hot dog man north of the boardwalk's pushed his cart to Queens by now. The Commissioner's calling it 'the greatest civic congregation since the agora of Athens.' Whatever that means."

"It means it's the priciest party taxpayers have ever foot the bill for, that's what it means," opines Lionel Bangs.

Paloma hands the jangling key ring over to the manager and says, "I hear they've got lousy rides at the World's Fair. A girl I know went last weekend. She says aside from a carousel and some slow-as-molasses rowboats, there's nothing much in the way of rides. I don't care how shiny and pretty it is – I don't see how anyone could pick a Fair without dodge 'em cars over Luna Park or the Pavilion of Fun."

26

"Don't speak too soon, missy," replies Ramsey. "I heard over the transom they moved a slew of amusements in last weekend including a waddyacallit — Parachute Jump, yeah, that's it – sounds like a doozy of a thrill ride. Something we don't got..."

"What's a Parachute Jump?" asks Paloma.

Ramsey widens his stance and pulls his hands from his belt to demonstrate. "This 'ting is a two-hundred-foot tower contraption. Looks like the Eiffel Tower, see, only with a tambourine on its top. It hoists you up, see, and then it drops you from a parachute. Pretty darn authentic-o, if you know what I mean."

"You a paratrooper, Officer Ramsey?" asks Paloma innocently.

The policeman splutters and sucks in his sizable gut.

"Didn't quite make the cut, sweetheart," he coughs.

The cop falls silent and then wipes at his face as if trying to erase the amusement from it.

"All right then, back to the base. I gotta find some leads to follow. If I fill out another report with the cold case bureau, I'm likely to get suspended. Who could lose four kids? And not a single doggone lead?"

Officer Ramsey scratches his head and adds, "Least not one that checks out."

"Well listen, Officer, don't you worry about Luna Park. I've brought on double security shifts, so's to keep watch," says Lionel. "Don't know how I'll pay 'em without ticket sales. But safety first, right?"

"That's right. And I appreciate it, Lionel. I do. If I could just get that kind of cooperation from that low-life Mingus Lamont over at Steeplechase Park. He'd sooner feed one of his junk-yard dogs filet mignon than hire some extra security for his Pavilion of Fun, the cheapskate."

Ramsey scowls in the direction of the huge park sprawling catty-corner from Luna Park on the other side of Surf Avenue. Together, they are like Coney Island royalty: Luna is Coney's Queen, her heart and soul, while Steeplechase is the funny bone – the King that's also a joker. Officer Ramsey doesn't often express himself poetically. But everyone knows that he does pick favorites, and that there's no love lost between him and Steeplechase Park's shifty new manager, Mingus Lamont.

Now Officer Ramsey turns to size up Luna's youngest loyalists. Paloma, despite the pinwheel in her strawberry blonde hair, is hands-on-hips-business. Buff, shorter by a head, grips the straps of his rucksack and looks the cop in the eye. Ramsey feels reassured.

"Can't say why, but somehow I'm not worried about the two of youse," he says with a smile. "All the same, promise me you'll be extra sharp now, see? Make sure somebody knows your wherareyabouts at all times, see? Doc Couney. Lionel, here. Yer ma, Paloma."

Paloma nods. She doesn't say that her mother could be down the block or in Atlantic City and might be home by dinnertime or not till next Tuesday. She doesn't say that she's had to be sharp since she was an infant, thank you very much, and she won't stop now.

"Sure, Officer," is all she says.

Buff waits until Ramsey has nearly reached the gate before he runs to catch up.

"Officer Ramsey?"

"Yeah, kid?"

Buff starts and then stops. He wonders what to say.

"What's up?" prompts the policeman.

"I think I saw the girl. Mary Lou. But not where she went. Just, you know, I think maybe I saw her sometime yesterday."

Ramsey pulls a notebook from his shirt pocket and licks the tip of his pencil. "Tell me."

Buff is silent. What is there to tell?

She was surprised.

Surprised by sadness.

She disappeared.

He starts to explain – about the hole in the board-walk. A void that was once just a small hole poked in the

29

fabric of fun, but that spread and spread and swallowed her whole.

Buff stops. Ramsey is looking at him quizzically. He's not writing anything down. Buff stammers, then remembers the doll. He hastily pulls his rucksack off and opens the flap. He takes out the rag doll and hands it to the cop, who holds it wonderingly. Something flies across the grown man's face and leaves him looking foolish. As if, for a moment, he thought he had found the blond girl with pigtails and had lifted her to safety.

"Okay, Buff," Ramsey says finally. "Maybe this will help. Come see me if you remember anything else."

Overhead, two banks of clouds part just enough to display a patch of pale blue sky. Buff lifts his eyes and sees there the moon, wan and watchful, hiding in the daylight. He can even see the profile of its shadowed dark side, like a frame of silver wire. Then, just as quickly as they opened, the clouds draw tight over the sky. Hiding again the hidden moon, and the hidden moon's hidden dark side. So many layers of invisibility.

This is the problem, he thinks. *The moon does not disappear. It just goes dark.*

The children are not gone; they are just hidden.

On the other side of visible.

Again, Buff sees the girl's face, sees her cast her eyes downward to the puddle of melting ice cream at her feet, sees her father turn his back on her, her mother join him, the girl become invisible. He sees the doll, dropped, forgotten.

Mother?

The tune in his head grows louder, and the words are clear: *Ring around the luna, Ring around the luna.*

"What was that all about?" Paloma is at the boy's shoulder, watching Ramsey walking down Surf Avenue with a rag doll swinging from his hand like a forgotten appendage.

"Our first clue," says Buff.

As he says it, he believes it. The children must be found. They have gone missing so that they can be found.

"We need to make a perimeter all the way around Luna Park and search its entire circumference," he explains. He's forgotten all about his story-telling booth and its lack of customers. He's forgotten about promises made both to Henry and Ramsey. He is thinking only of the unfinished tune, which is buzzing at double speed in his ears. "We need to make a ring around Luna."

Paloma does a cartwheel and lets out an excited whoop.

"Let's start at the creek."

CHAPTER SIX

Far from Brooklyn, a tall man with broad shoulders and the profile of a hawk stands at a wall of windows. From his skyscraper perch, he is inspecting, not watching, the sluggish grey river that is Manhattan's own moat.

The man is the Parks Commissioner, but his title doesn't suggest what his hard jaw and hooded eyes do: he is the most powerful man in the city.

The Parks Commissioner? you might say. The most powerful man in New York City?

Indeed, no one would have guessed it four years ago when he grasped the Mayor's hand and posed for the newsboys' cameras in a gloomy side-room in City Hall. Though he towered above the famously rotund mayor, no one in the room looked at the silver-haired appointee and figured him for the next boss. No one, that is, but the brand new Parks Commissioner himself, who didn't blink once against the cameras' flashbulbs. He had other stars in his eyes.

He was the first to see it — that Parks are Power. That in the dense and expanding city, open space is gold. It can buy the public, and it can sell a hunch. It is terra firma for star-spangled dreams, and four years after taking control of the parks the Commissioner has seen a great dream come true.

Now he clasps his hands behind his back and surveys his dominion. His sharp eyes linger on his proudest landmark – the glinting globe and soaring spire across the river, reflecting sunlight all the way from Flushing, Queens. The Trylon and Perisphere, they are called. The Trylon soars into the future; the Perisphere, a perfect orb free of flaws and quirks, represents home base. A perfect planet.

The Commissioner allows himself a grim smile. He is satisfied with his work. He has transformed the abandoned wetlands of Flushing into a World's Fairgrounds. He has bulldozed the bushes and manicured the meadows. He has erected classical temples devoted to science, technology, industry and progress. He has brought "The World of Tomorrow" to New York, and in the month since the gates opened, the World's Fair has proved to be a popular world in which to spend a day and your dollars.

Now he shifts his gaze south, past the bridges spanning the river, towards the low reaches of Brooklyn. Somewhere on that soupy horizon is another landmark. Another beacon of a popular playground. But today, Coney Island's Wonder Wheel hides from the Commissioner's scrutiny.

"Goodbye, Coney Island," he says scornfully. "And good riddance."

It was just over a year ago that the Commissioner emerged from the back of a somber black car speckled with the mud of Ocean Parkway to announce that he was now in charge of Coney Island.

"It is time for the People's Playground to be returned to the people," he had thundered from a makeshift podium on the boardwalk. "The legendary lore of Coney Island, tainted by con-men and hucksters, carnies and crooks, has run its course. Utterly. Rather than invest in its continued state of squalid entertainment, the city has chosen to oversee the natural demise of this decrepit amusement park and restore the shore to a salubrious state of public benefit."

Then the Commissioner posted new rules and regulations, ordered a crew to begin measuring the beach and signaled to his poker-faced driver that it was time to depart.

"Apparently we ain't the people," muttered Cheeks the Human Bullfrog, once the dust from the Commissioner's departure had settled. "He thinks if he builds picket fences and pay toilets and plants tulips everywhere, the carnies are gonna slink off into the night. But he's got another think coming."

In fact, the Commissioner had not returned to Coney Island since that day. Indeed, as Cheeks suggested, he had other things to think about. He had his own playground to build. One in which rigor replaced razzle-dazzle and civility trumped crowds. The Commissioner is proud of his World of Tomorrow — a popular destination free of magic booths and games of chance, unadorned with whirly gigs and contortionists; a family fair without a single circus freak or dodge 'em car.

But it still itches – that his World of Tomorrow has left room in its orbit for the crazy, careening Coney Island.

On the large desk behind him, the morning paper lies open with an item on the crime blotter outlined in the thick red pen: Another Child Goes Missing in Coney Island.

The intercom on the deck buzzes.

"What is it," he says. There is no question mark in his voice.

"The Steeplechase man is here to see you," says the disembodied voice of his secretary.

"Send him in."

The double doors of the Commissioner's office open. Mingus Lamont, the slightly cross-eyed manager of Steeplechase Park, walks in with his hat in his hands.

"Thank you for coming," says the Commissioner. "I realize you are a busy man with many responsibilities." He covers his mouth and coughs as though the words he has just spoken have stuck in his throat.

"Oh, well, Commissioner," says Lamont, with a smile that tries to be charming and fails. "There's not so much to be done down at Coney, aside from, of course, your business. I mean it's practically the off-season, what with your World's Fair hitting its stride."

"Now, Mr. Lamont," replies the Commissioner, raising his hand as if to stop the conversation. "There is much work to be done down in your neighborhood, as you well know. I will be moving ahead with my revitalization plans for Coney Island just as soon as the World's Fair closes, but it will take a great deal of preliminary work on the ground for the project to be a success. It will take the cooperation and diligence of men like yourself. Men with intimate knowledge of the ... obstacles we face."

The Commissioner pauses and allows the Coney Island carny a moment to nod his agreement.

"Of course, once we begin, Mr. Lamont, you will no longer be troubled with the concerns that you now deal with daily – no more brawls to break up; no more storms to clean up after; no more carting away unpopular rides only to find that now they are gone, everyone wants them back..."

Mingus Lamont laughs and turns his hat in his hands. "Yup, that's about it, Mr. Commissioner. And don't forget the elephant dung and the drunks and the kids who squeeze through the fence at night. Plus there's the fireworks to keep dry and the towels to launder and half the freak show wanting a discount on their day off. No sir, I'm looking forward to a nice quiet Coney Island free of the riff-raff and the hoopla. I'll be just fine without the roller coasters – some days up and some days down and you just never know what's gonna happen down there…"

Mingus Lamont swallows hard, choking down the words that threaten to spill out. Words like – me, me, me, and my turn. For though he is a thoroughly bad apple, the Steeplechase boss is also a decent judge of character. He sees that the Commissioner has no patience for impatient men and trusts nobody's certainty but his own. Lamont knows he will grasp greatness only by groveling. To be King of Coney, he must first be a toady. Luckily, it is a role that comes naturally to Mingus Lamont.

The Commissioner steps to the desk and picks up a long blue slip. He hands it to Lamont, who grabs it a little too quickly and scans the numbers on it greedily. He smiles crookedly. "That's real generous of you Mr. Commissioner, sir. I see you put a bit extra on the top there so you must be pleased with what I've sent you."

"Oh indeed. The metal is top-notch, evidently free of rust and defects. My engineers tell me it's just the thing for our reinforcements. We've connected the Trylon to the Perisphere, you know, with the longest escalator in the world. It requires constant maintenance. The turf you provided, also, is very high-quality." He gives a snort. "And to think that it was originally meant for Steeplechase Park, where a bunch of ill-behaved children would tear it to shreds in a matter of days. Absolutely criminal misuse. You were quite correct to ... reroute it my way."

Mingus Lamont pulls his one lazy eyeball away from the check to focus on his new benefactor. He recalls how the other carnies had dismissed the Commissioner, waving him away like any run-of-the-mill bureaucrat from City Hall.

"This place'll spit him out like sand from a clam," is what that smart-alec Handsome Henry had said.

Well, thinks the Steeplechase manager with a sneer, *who's spitting now?*

"But actually," continues the Commissioner, "the extra you see on the check is not so much for goods delivered as for future resources." He taps the open newspaper with a frown. "I have been thinking about these children. The ones that keep getting themselves lost down at Coney Island."

"Oh yes sir, terrible tragedy that," offers Mingus Lamont. "And a nuisance too," he adds, hedging his bets.

The Commissioner looks up from the paper and levels his cold eyes on the carny. "I rather think it could be the nail in the coffin for old Coney Island," he says. "I mean, really. As if it's not enough to endure the long subway ride, the intolerable crowds, the rowdies and the clowns and the come-ons and the blaring noise..."

"Oh that's gotten much better, sir," interjects Lamont. "Ever since you confiscated the megaphones and banned the barkers."

"New York's families deserve a dignified day of leisure," continues the Commissioner, who is a great champion of leisure even if he never partakes of it himself. "For New York's families, who deserve a healthy day of outdoor exercise and an affordable dose of erudition and wonder, Coney Island is a sham. A sad excuse for a park. A disgrace and an insult to the good people of this city."

The Commissioner pauses and taps the paper again with a long finger.

"And it is also a danger. If families don't recognize this, they should be made to recognize it. I would not be at all surprised if this... trend...should escalate. If this rash of abductions, disappearances...should continue."

Mingus Lamont is not aware of his open mouth as the Commissioner closes the newspaper and studies his visitor closely.

"You've been an efficient and discreet partner, Mingus," he says. "I'm asking you to see to it that these disappearances make, shall we say, a great impact on Coney Island's most obstinate loyalists. They should not forget the grief that grows in the heart of unbridled amusement.

They should become acquainted with the dark underbelly of that so-called funpark."

Mingus Lamont continues to stand slack-jawed in the middle of the room. Even his restless hands are still.

"You will be well rewarded," says the Commissioner. Then he rises and escorts the little man to the door.

When it closes behind him, Lamont turns and studies the knots in the hewn wood. He scratches his greasy head, repeating to himself the words that have just passed on the other side. Then he gives a yelp of recognition. It sounds, to the Parks Commissioner's secretary, like the cry of a small animal in a trap.

CHAPTER SEVEN

Coney Island Creek emerges from Gravesend Bay and creeps east for about two miles before disappearing entirely under the hulks and sandbars behind Luna Park. It's a malodorous stream, appealing only to migratory water birds and treasure-hunting kids. It's also a natural spot to look for bodies, booby-traps, and deflated beach-balls. Buff and Paloma are discussing what, exactly, they should be on the lookout for.

"European types. They're awful suspicious, aren't they?" suggests Paloma. "Sinister. And funnier-dressers than even the sideshow freaks. Turbans and what not. We should look for turbans. Discarded in flight."

"You've been listening to too much 'Little Orphan Annie.' I'm pretty sure she's the only kid getting kidnapped by sheikhs and Portuguese gorilla hunters. Anyway, sheikhs aren't European. They're arabite."

"Whatever they are, if they think they can start marauding down here in Brooklyn, they got another think coming."

Buff smiles at his friend's fighting pose. Nothing scares

Paloma Bright — not the roughnecks who yell at her pretty mother when they walk down the Bowery, not the undertow near the Dreamland Pier, not the crazy spider crabs that wash in like a whole crabby army after storms. Buff has seen Paloma stand up to Omar the one-eyed bladesman and heard her sass McShane, the three-and-a-half-foot-tall jail-keeper of Lilliputia who's so mean he once locked his own mother up for calling him a knucklehead. Nobody sasses McShane. He keeps a box of trained rats.

Buff figures Paloma is hoping to discover the kidnapper just so she can give him a piece of her mind. But she surprises him.

"It's not just radio-land, Buff," she says seriously. "It's in all the papers too. Europe's just chock full of folks running and chasing each other."

True enough, thinks Buff.

Every day forces aligning.

Armies invading.

Governments betraying.

People fleeing.

That's far away, though, across the ocean. Over in Europe, where Doc's from. In fact, where Doc's from, a whole darn country got gobbled up not so long ago by that German general – an angry little man with floppy hair who always looks ready to crack up in the newsreels, shrieking silently before the movies begin. Doc says he just marched across into someone else's stomping grounds and said Mine. Or maybe *Mein.*

Buff considers for a moment the things that could make a man want to kidnap a whole country. *What happens to the people of a place that goes missing?* He wonders. *Do they go missing too?* A new fear creeps up his neck – not for himself or for the kids of Coney Island, but for Coney itself. He thinks of the Commissioner – a man whose face he can no longer remember, but whose somber black car he can still see descending on Surf Avenue like a vulture. His home, he thinks, is under siege.

"Buff, look at yerself! You're standing in the middle of the road, for Pete's sake."

Buff hurries across the street to where Paloma stands shaking her head. "The heck you doing? Measuring your shadow?"

"Yep. And then multiplying it by 3.14."

"Why 3.14?"

"You know. Basic geometry. Calculating the circumference. Three point one four is Pi."

"Pie comes later, geometry boy," says Paloma, tugging him by the hand onto the footpath to the ramshackle dock on Coney Island creek known to the locals as the "marina."

There are three vessels to be seen in the marina – all of them belonging to a man with questionable navigation skills and the nickname Cap'n Clyde. On the bank is a rowboat too full of fishnets to board. Lashed to the dock is an inflatable raft in which Clyde gives occasional tours to the occasional Scandinavian tourist. "Only a proper Viking can appreciate its seaworthiness," he says. The third craft, moored on the other side of the dock, is a bona fide boat – a twenty-foot dinghy with a cabin, steering wheel, and sidewinder pole holders. She's called the Mickey.

Clyde has been promising Buff and Paloma an open-water cruise on the Mickey for close to five years now. That's how long he's been scouring the funparks for spare mechanicals to give his prize vessel "more gumption," by which he means a motor that would carry the boat beyond the mouth of the creek.

"Just a few more improvements and the Mick will be a regular naiad of the deep," he often says, to which Paloma replies, "That's what we're afraid of — the very, very deep — as in the bottom of the sea."

"Ahoy there," Clyde calls now. He's a wiry figure in a yellow rain hat and he's perched on the half-built cabin of the Mick. "A coupl'a salts come to join me at sea?"

"Actually, we thought we might lend Officer Ramsey a little help. With his search," replies Buff.

Clyde frowns at that. "Aye. Can't say as I don't step a bit more gingerly through the shallows myself these days. Peek under more tarpaulins too. Every bundle I see bobbing down the creek gives me a touch o' the willies."

The self-proclaimed Captain sits back on his haunches and rubs his stubbled chin. There seem to be extra clouds in his rheumy eyes.

"I'm afraid the Mick needs a wee bit o' work before I can take 'er out today. But there's a perfectly good little vessel right here that will give us some legs in our look-see," he says. "Come on aboard."

Buff and Paloma slide down the bank and into the rubber raft. Clyde hands them both a paddle and positions his long frame in the stern. He pulls a battered sailor's hat from under a box of bait and replaces the rain hat on his head. Paloma and Buff steer the little boat into the middle of the creek and head west, scanning the shore for clues – signs of struggle, a trail gone dead, or maybe a hasty SOS message.

Ten minutes pass before they encounter anything out of the ordinary on the creek: a waterlogged case of Dr. Brown's Cel-Ray soda barely keeping afloat. Clyde hauls the box on board, causing the raft to ride significantly lower in the water. Paloma is just beginning to complain of the damp when suddenly there is a ripping sound, a gasping sound, and the sound of Clyde hollering "all hands on deck, major breach at the fo'castle hull!"

What appears to be a mattress spring is now adorning the front of the raft like a figurehead.

"Abandon ship!" calls Clyde as Coney Island Creek oozes into the raft.

Buff is the first to reach the bank. Paloma joins him, squeezing the creek from her socks. Clyde is chest-deep, valiantly collecting Cel-Ray soda into the raft's reduced hold. "We may need it when the tide turns and leaves us becalmed for days with nothin' to quench the thirst but the creek and me whiskey!" he shouts.

Buff assures Clyde that it's a wise precaution, and that he will follow the drifting raft from the bank "to scout against Cel-Ray thieves."

Picking his way downstream through the bushes, Buff is soon distracted by the dense green honeysuckle thickets growing wild on along the bank. He's sipping on his fourth plucked blossom when he notices something poking out from under a bush. It's a large piece of canvas covered in rust-colored stains.

He hesitates.

He pulls it out.

It's child-size.

Buff's heart sticks in his throat. He imagines the bruised knees and scraped elbows poking the canvas shroud into its heart-breaking shape. He moves to unfold it but falters again when a cloud of flies rise from the awful bundle. Stumbling backwards, he calls to Paloma, who whacks her way through the honeysuckle to Buff's side.

He points wordlessly. The two children stand frozen for several seconds before the girl steps forward, grabs the canvas, and pulls.

Buff's eyes are squeezed shut.

"Oh for crying out loud," he hears Paloma say.

Buff opens his eyes and sees a broken-down picnic basket, four empty lemonade bottles, and a ketchup-stained blanket. Paloma crosses her arms and glares at Buff, but can't suppress a giggle.

"Let's scram, before Clyde has us patching up the Mick with scotch tape," she says.

CHAPTER EIGHT

Mingus Lamont checks his watch. He has hurried back from the Commissioner's office to Steeplechase Park, uncharacteristically eager for a crowd worthy of a mid-summer morning. There isn't one. Not yet. But they will come. They've been coming since opening day, much to the park manager's disgust.

Just last week a clankety omnibus showed up at the gates, loaded with grubby orphans from some sad sack home in the city. The bus had fairly jumped off the ground, though it was parked and braked. That's how excited the brats were to find themselves outside the Steeplechase Park Pavilion of Fun. Lamont had barely made it to the gate in time. Barely managed to unroll the notice that was taped on the ticket booth, curled up like a scroll from the heat. But he unrolled it, he did, and addressed the presumptuous ninny who had led the charge.

"Says right here in big bold letters you can read with those glasses sittin' on yer face," he had pointed out helpfully. Then he read it out loud. Slowly. Word by word: LARGE. GROUPS. BY. RESERVATION. ONLY.

The ninny lost some of her bossiness at that, he recalls now. She pushed her spectacles up high on her nose, looked around at the children, who were already tussling and rolling about on the browning grass and said, "But they're all quite small."

But Mingus Lamont never broke the rules. At least not the rules he made. "By reservation only, lady. Wanna make a reservation for tomorrow?"

She didn't. So the kids all loaded back into the bus and the bus fired up its engine and trundled down the road to Luna Park. "Good riddance," Lamont had muttered after firing the ticket taker who had nearly allowed a kiddy convention in his funpark. He had other plans for Steeplechase, which he recognized as an excellent supply depot for the World of Tomorrow.

But that was last week.

This week Mingus Lamont would have welcomed all of Brooklyn's snot-nosed kids. This week the Steeplechase manager has a whole new business plan. "Should that trend continue," he says now, imitating the Commissioner's pompous phrasing.

It's been just over two months since the ugly little man with the lazy eye got called in on short notice to run Coney Island's biggest funpark. Since then, Lamont's effect on the park has been quick and stinging. He has learned exactly how much screw tightening could be postponed and just how many bathhouse tiles could be left unreplaced. He has managed to create a playground just run down enough to make cautious mothers think twice about putting their darlings on the swings, but not so decrepit that any of the injuries sustained couldn't be fixed up with a bandage, some iodine, and a lollipop.

"One of them licorice jobs that nobody likes anyhow," he specifies.

But if the park is losing its fans at an alarming pace, Lamont himself is quite pleased with the way things are going. It is not even the Fourth of July, and already he has made more money for himself than in any other summer on the circuit. There's no question about it– he has made a wise offer in arranging for some of the excess materials in the Steeplechase warehouse to be "re-routed" to the World's Fairgrounds in Flushing. Since then, Lamont has found all sorts of ways to be of service to the Parks Commissioner. And the Commissioner, Lamont knows full well, has more influence on Coney Island than all the carnies from the Bowery to Broadway.

And so, though he usually does his best to ignore them, today Mingus Lamont is watching his young patrons closely. He will spend the morning tracking them from the moment they tumble through the Bingo Barrel, swarming one ride after the next like a drone of hyperactive bees. When one of them drops back, distracted by a puppy on a leash or an errant balloon, Mingus will take special notice.

Now his crooked gaze follows a young mother trying to herd her four children through the House of Mirrors. He watches as her delight in her morphing, elongated children turns to surprise when they round the corner and not four, but twenty-four, children are holding her hand. He sees her amusement turn to alarm when she enters the tricky corridor where the littlest one appears to disappear altogether. He sees her relief, tinged with wariness, when the tyke is discovered walking upside down on the mirrored ceiling.

"Nail in the coffin should that trend continue," mutters Mingus Lamont. They are the words that have haunted him since he left the Commissioner's office.

A sour-looking youth in tight trousers and a collarless shirt slouches up next to the Steeplechase manager. An unlit cigarette dangles from the boy's mouth and a small chain hangs from his belt. At the end of the chain is a hook where a lucky rabbit's foot once hung. But this kid doesn't believe in good luck. Lamont picked him up outside the House of Detention over in Gravesend last week and offered him employment as "enhanced security." Then he sniggered and added "authorized by Officer Sherman

Ramsey himself."

"What's cookin', Lamont?" asks Snake in a surly voice.

"Lissen," says his stooped boss. "We need to round up some more manpower. Let's you and me go talk to some of yer no-account buddies. I gotta job for them."

Mingus Lamont has hatched a plan. It ricochets down the reflective corridors of the house of mirrors, bouncing like a bad idea.

CHAPTER NINE

Still damp from their escapade in the creek, Buff and Paloma climb onto a pair of stools in front of the lunch counter at Nedick's Drugstore.

"How about a story then," suggests Paloma as she considers the menu. "If I've never heard it before I'll go crazy and get egg salad. Otherwise, it's grilled cheese, as usual."

Buff thinks a moment. "I suppose you've heard about the tunnel? The Flushing tunnel?"

Paloma shakes her head. "No. Why don't you tell me about the Flushing tunnel."

"Well that's how Flushing got its name," begins Buff. "People call it wetlands, you know, and it is. There's so much water underground there, that the only way they keep it from overflowing and flooding all of Queens, is to suck it out like it was a giant pull chain toilet."

Paloma laughs. "I always said Queens stinks!"

"Now, the water, when it gets flushed, has to go somewhere. Gotta go to sea. So that's where it goes. There are very few people who know about the Flushing tunnel, and now you're one of them. When they pull that big chain, the bog water goes rushing through the tunnel and ends, where do you think?"

"In Coney Island Creek! That's why it smells like a boardwalk toilet!"

"But here's the thing," says Buff over Paloma's laughter. "Sometimes, the tunnel gets backed up. And now that they've plunked a fairgrounds in Flushing, there's almost more trash to be flushed than swamp water. Weeks worth of ticket stubs, flower garlands, maps and candy wrappers have gummed it all up, the tunnel. So every so often, they have to get out an enormous plunger. It's the size of a water tower, but with a big ol' sucker round its bottom. They put it over the Flushing entrance, fasten a pile driver to it, and whoosh! The tunnel is clear again. Only problem is, the force of the..." Buff flaps his hands, looking for a good term. "The force of the 'Interborough Super Suck' has been known to take with it small objects over on this side of the tunnel. Small, unfastened, unwary objects. Newspaper stands, ice carts, scooters, stray cats and even..."

Paloma is looking at Buff wide-eyed, as though she could actually see a small child standing in the middle of the World's Fair, wondering how Coney Island's higgledy-piggledy beachfront has turned into a campus of tended lawns and smooth asphalt.

"Buff," she begins. But Buff has imagined the same scene – children abandoned and lost in a World of Tomorrow. There would be worse places to be shanghaied to, he thinks, and is about to suggest it when he sees Paloma's excited face.

"The Interborough Super Suck," she intones, holding her face in her hands in mock horror. "The Black Hole of Brooklyn ... into its terrifying void goes trolley cars, soda fountains and families of unusually short stature."

It can transport fire engines, apartment buildings," adds Buff dramatically. "Not even the Brooklyn Dodgers are safe from its maw, in which all of the borough's treasures are fast disappearing!"

Paloma calls to the soda jerk at the other end of the counter. "Egg salad for me, Frankie. And a cheese sandwich for Buff and two chocolate egg creams. Also – a pencil."

"Your wish is my command," answers Frankie as he pulls a stub from behind his ear and hands it to Paloma with a wink. Most girls would have blushed at that, since Frankie has brilliantine hair, long eyelashes and is generally considered "hotsy-totsy." But Paloma just looks at him like maybe he has a tic.

"We've got to get serious if we're going to find anything today," she says to Buff. "I mean it ain't gonna happen like in the movies. You know - how the gumshoe is sitting at the lunch counter scratching his head over the clues that don't fit together and then all of a sudden he sees a suspicious character walking by looking all... suspicious, so he throws down a nickel and takes off after him and chases him into traffic and the guy is dead before he can even come to justice. I mean, that would be nice and all. But it ain't gonna happen that way."

Buff turns to look out the dirty plate-glass window at the decidedly unsuspicious passage of pedestrians among the storefront awnings of Neptune Avenue. Across the street, Mr. Gilchrest the greengrocer is arranging apples in a pyramid. Next door, the butcher is sweeping sawdust into the street. He watches their small habits, noticing what they don't - that they are moving together in their own little worlds.

Like synchronized swimmers.

Or synchronized sweepers.

The neighbors of Neptune Avenue...

Sweeping in solidarity.

The butcher passes the broom to Mr. Gilchrest and Buff, still watching that small moment on Neptune Avenue, says: "Right. We need to be, you know ... systematic."

Paloma flips her paper place mat over and begins a list of her favorite Coney Island hiding spots: "Ravenhall, Stauch's and the other bath houses; the machine room at the Cyclone, since I noticed there's a new lock on it; the stables behind the subway, the dodgem' car hanger; the Blue Grotto next to the Bobsled, I guess — wonder if we could borrow the frog-man's wetsuit?"

Paloma is scribbling rapidly, sucking down one of Frankie's superior egg creams as she does.

"The old Playland arcade, of course," adds Buff.

"What's left of it. You been in since after the fire?" asks Paloma. "I've only been in that one time, when the ground was still hot and the rails were gooey. But I don't think anybody ever cleared out the mess. It's worth a look."

Buff is thinking again about the moon and what hides on its dark side. The other side of visible, he thinks and then says, louder: "Backstage at Loews theater. Behind the screen."

Paloma nods and adds the movie theater to the list. Frankie returns with sandwiches and a bowl of pickles.

"Frankie, you know all those kids gone missing on Coney?" asks Paloma between bites. "Did you see any of them come in here before they disappeared?"

"Could be," says Frankie. "But I don't guess any of them was cute enough or clever enough for me to pay much attention."

He tousles Paloma's hair, which she tolerates briefly before announcing, "Frankie, if you were any more of a flirt, I imagine your tongue would just dissolve in its spit like sugar."

Frankie hoots at this. "Paloma, isn't there anything I can do to win your heart?"

"Yes. We need to see in the walk-in icebox."

The soda jerk shrugs, pulls off his apron and leads the them out the front door and down a side alley to the shed where all the ham, eggs, ice cream and milk are stored.

Paloma makes an exhaustive search of the premises, but finds nothing more interesting than the shell of a horseshoe crab and a single bathing shoe stuck in a slick of half-frozen syrup. Buff wonders at the prints on the butter, small indentations the size of a cat's tongue. Frankie is about to lock up again when he stops with a grunt. He scratches his head and then begins counting boxes on a high shelf.

"I coulda sworn that we got a shipment of hot dogs on Monday. There should be fifteen crates, but I only see eight. I better check with Mr. Nedick on that," he says.

When Frankie shuts the door and snaps the padlock back into place Buff notices a gash near the hinge. It's about the size of one of the lathes they use at Steeplechase when a mechanical horse derails and needs to get jacked. He points it out.

"Yep," says Frankie. "I do believe we've had an icebox breach."

"That's a fiendish cat," mutters Buff.

Paloma disagrees. After all, she's invited dozens of

tabbies and toms to supper. They're good company on nights when her mother is out. "Any cat worth keeping," she says, making a note on her folded placemat, "knows how to help himself to the milk.

"C'mon, Buff," she says. "We've got a lot of ground to cover." Buff exchanges a bemused look with Frankie, pulls some change from his pocket for the half-eaten sandwiches, and hurries after his partner, who is already headed south to Surf Avenue.

The Sea Geekery, a ramshackle building two blocks from Nedick's, bills itself as a "Marine Menagerie." The sign at on the door promises to reveal ALL THE MYSTER- IES OF THE DEEP OR YOUR DIME YOU CAN KEEP Buff and Paloma pass the boy snoozing boy in the ticket window and enter the dank gallery. They examine the two-headed octopus, the albino starfish and the solid gold anchor wordlessly, but when they reach the end of the hall where the supposed remains of the Half Moon sit heavily in the gloom, Paloma clambers on deck and declares for the umpteenth time: "There's no way this is Henry Hudson's ship. It wouldn't cross my bathtub, let alone the Atlantic!"

Buff is about to respond when another voice beats him to it.

"The Half Moon's but a ghost ship now."

Greta Gershwin, the mysterious woman who lives

above the Sea Geekery and keeps her telescope trained on the horizon day and night, is standing in the corner. As always, she's a startling sight – a bent-back crone with smooth skin and jet-black hair.

"The Half Moon lives on the bottom of the sea, where all of the roots of this island lead. This one ..." (Greta steps forward and kicks the hull of the ship with surprising force) "is a skeleton. Bones of a legend, blood of a myth."

Paloma jumps from the flimsy structure and feigns new interest in the legendary ruin.

"Ships today come to less good fortune than even this one," Greta continues. She pulls a ratty cloak closer over her shoulders. "The Half Moon was fated to tragedy. Insubordination. Mutiny. But the ship captains today? No better. They are taking Coney's gold once again. Bringing misery in as ballast."

The strange woman sidles up to Buff, close enough so that he can see the white streak of her scalp under her dark hair.

"It will go down too," she says, her voice clear as an iron bell. "It will sink to the bottom, taking its cargo with it."

"What will?" asks Buff, uneasy.

"The Miasma. The Miasma will go down to the bottom. If we're lucky."

Then Greta Gershwin pulls a writhing brown paper bag from under her cloak. Mesmerized, Buff and Paloma watch as she extracts a long red sea-worm from the bag and eyes it dispassionately.

"Snack?" she offers, as she drops the finger-length creature down her throat.

Buff is the first to the exit.

CHAPTER TEN

It is late afternoon and Buff and Paloma have crossed off most of the spots on Paloma's list: Manny's arcade had provided little in the way of clues; just a fine fifteen minutes' worth of skeeball. The box-o-rama was closed up tight due to a welterweight fight over in Jersey between the reigning champs, Big Guy Stuyvesant and Georgie the Fly. The only living thing in the velodrome was a flock off bedraggled pigeons.

Buff was particularly disappointed to find nothing in the stuffy catwalk behind the screen at Loew's Theater. It had seemed like such an inspired idea, even if Paloma didn't quite get what he was trying to say about the other side of visible. "Shadow hunting, Buff? Is that what you think we should be doing?"

"I'm just saying that sometimes things hide in plain day. Like the moon. It's still in the sky, just hidden by the sun. And its dark side too."

"The moon, huh." Paloma stoops to pick up a noise-maker in the weeds. She pulls its ragged string and it lets out a quack.

"Tell me something, Buff," she says, "What's another word for moon?"

Buff thinks for a moment and slaps his forehead.

"Luna," he says. "Luna is Latin for moon."

Paloma nods. "And you're the one gets A's in school."

Buff hums under his breath: *Ring around the Luna.* He cranes his neck, but there are no marks on the skin of the sky. He looks back down Surf Avenue, towards Luna Park. *What sort of stakeout makes a ring around Luna?* He scans the landscape: the Norton Point trolley turns a corner up ahead. Beyond that, there are only parallel lines – Surf Avenue, the boardwalk, the ocean and the horizon. Buff can just see the water – slate grey and unimpressed by what, on a good summer day, would be called the golden hour but today can only be called leaden.

"And speaking of Latin," says Paloma. "What was that crazy Greta at the Sea Geekery on about 'miasma'?"

"It means something like swamp. Miasma makes it hard to breathe, hard to move. Molasses weather."

"Like all summer."

"Yeah. Exactly. I don't know if it's Latin. But definitely ancient-y. You know, how maybe it's the gods who cook up miasma up in their Olympus kitchen. Then they let it ooze down all over us mere mortals."

"Mortals," Paloma snickers. "Listen to you: *mortals, miasma.*"

"Miasmortals," riffs Buff. "Destined for extinction at the end of the Miasmepoch. The Great Miasmera."

"Well, I'm all for an end to it," says Paloma with a sniff at the murky funk of humidity. She gives the noise-maker another quack for emphasis. "I don't need no more stinkin' miasma."

They trudge on in silence, wondering. Instinctively they turn right towards the boardwalk, where heavy sky is heaviest. Paloma collapses onto a bench, the same one that Buff had sat on to put on his shoes after his swim this morning. The same one where he had heard about Mary Lou Walker. The same one that had sheltered a forgotten rag doll. He leans back on the bench and lets his eyes drift over a horizon that is barely distinguishable between the wet grey water and the slate grey sky. Far to the west he can just make out a solitary freighter moving slowly towards the Point. He sniffs the soft stench of sulphur.

"Wonder what she meant about Coney's gold being carried off."

"Greta? Who knows. She's a loony. And her ship, too. Loony ship."

"Luna ship," mumbles Buff.

Ring around the Luna. Ring around the Luna. Ashes, ashes... we all fall ...

"Come on," he says, turning his back on the sea.

Paloma follows Buff down the stairs and they walk

in silence towards the funparks. Soon they see the Norton Point trolley approaching, headed west. A clang from behind tells them the eastbound trolley is just as near. Stepping out of the street, the friends watch the pair of trolleys cross paths directly in front of Steeplechase Park. And something else happens at the intersection: from each of the cars, two figures - fare-busters judging from the practiced way they hang from the poles in the back of the cars – jump to the street.

"Safe landing!" shouts Paloma. But when the four figures turn to her voice, she sucks in her breath. They are a study in intimidation – a foursome of tough customers, body language all threats and grudges. And each of them is wearing a mask - the mask of the Funny Face mascot of Steeplechase Park, the grinning, demented dandy with his all-seeing eyes. The effect is instantly alarming.

Buff grabs Paloma's arm instinctively. "Ow," she whispers, but not because of his grip.

Frozen, Buff and Paloma watch the four Funny Faces slink-strut across Surf Avenue. into Steeplechase Park.

"The heck is that all about?" Buff turns to Paloma, expecting a salty assessment, but she just gives a brief shudder and looks up at the sky.

"I wanna go home," she says. "Getting dark."

And that worries Buff even more than the creepy new arrivals. Because he knows that there is only one thing that can frighten his fearless friend. It doesn't show itself often, since she lives above a Bowery dancehall that doesn't sleep till sunrise – but Paloma Bright, incubator baby, is truly afraid of the dark. Never before has Buff been reminded of Paloma's only fear during the summer season. But here it is, not even July, and already his friend is feeling Coney's autumn.

"Is your ma home?" he asks as they turn onto the Bowery. What he means is, is Louisa Bright downstairs at Bettleman's, dancing to put food on the table? Or is she somewhere else, confusing sweet-talkers with good-guys and rockgut with champagne? Paloma's mother is a pretty dancer and she sings sweet too. But Buff knows she has trouble keeping track of time, which is maybe why Paloma was born two months too soon.

"I'll be okay," smiles Paloma. "Really."

She scoops up a tabby-cat from the railing of the narrow steps that lead to her small apartment and perches the purring creature on her shoulder.

Fortified, she says, "Tomorrow we check Steeplechase."

Buff smiles, encouraged by Paloma's resolve. But his good mood leaves the moment she closes the door behind her. Because Steeplechase Park, home of the legendary Pavilion of Fun, is housing something un-fun. Something broody and bullying.

Steeplechase, thinks Buff, squinting down the darkening Bowery to the wire fence that encloses the park, is Luna's hidden dark side.

Waning Moon
June 21, 1939

*T*here is no barker at the end of the Dreamland Pier. No top-hatted impresario to announce: LADIES AND GENTLEMEN, STEP RIGHT UP TO SEE THE MATERNAL MARINE MIRACLE! IT S COLD AND IT S DEEP BUT IT S WORTH THE SWIM! JUST A NICKEL AND A DEEP BREATH WILL GET YOU AS CLOSE AS YOU LIKE TO A REAL MERMAID QUEEN! DON T FORGET TO LINGER WHEN YOU LEAVE OR YOU LL GET THE BENDS SURE AS A CORKSCREW!

But she is real, the Mermother. Not real like the dog boy or the pinhead or the Wild Man of Borneo, made real by the bally-man.The Mermother is real without witnesses to say so.

She lives in a grotto beneath the Dreamland Pier, the one that drowned during the great fire of 1911, when all the marvels of Dreamland went up in flame and came down in ash. When the fire licked the pier, it snapped in two, leaving the carousel and the small observatory that had perched on its far end gently on the ocean floor.

That same night, the Mermother arrived. She chose the den under the carousel top for her parlor and the shell of the soot-stained observatory for her boudoir. For years now, she has measured the health of Coney Island. She takes its pulse from the waves. From the sunken telescope she peers into the windows and the hearts of the seaside community. Physical contact with Coney Islanders has always been rare – once in a blue moon, bored or just playful, she might tickle the stray foot of a rowdy youngster who has cannonballed deep off the buoy platform. But tonight, for the first time since she claimed the underwater den, the Mermother has guests. They sleep on four fresh beds of seaweed. She turns her attention to the peculiar sound of soft snoring under water and hears a missing note. Someone is awake. From the pile of elbows and knees under the carousel top, a pair of eyes is watching her closely.

The Mermother crooks a finger and the blue eyes widen and dart from side to side before rising to reveal the slender neck and shoulders of a young girl in untidy braids. The child points a thumb to her chest and wordlessly mouths, "Me?"

The Mermother smiles and nods.

The girl stands, stretches, and steps lightly over the other sleeping figures. She has forgotten how she came to be in such strange company. She has forgotten her dismay when she pushed her tongue too hard against the ice cream and watched it land, plop, on the ground next to its upside down cone. She has forgotten the words her father hissed about the money dripping like ice cream through the boardwalk planks. She has forgotten how he stomped away without a backward glance and how her mother shook her head sadly and followed him.

But she remembers the sickening feeling of being left all alone. She remembers the ground giving way below her.

And then suddenly she was here, in this wavy, cool grotto where it smells of salty sunshine. There are others too – the boy from Chicago who was visiting relatives while his mother looked for work; a younger tyke who wears bruises from a forgotten incident; a lad, big and strong, who swims like a fish ... but disappeared under the waves anyway because his folks, weary after a week of too many worries, warned, "Don't go out too far, 'cause we ain't coming after ya."

These are the children who left no trace when they tumbled into holes on the Coney Island boardwalk – soft spots where despair has weakened the planks. Each one of them stumbled when support gave way; each had fallen because they were dropped. Each of them landed in the open arms of the Mermother.

Now they are four. Four children safe in an underwater limbo. They sing songs, play games. Ashes, ashes, we all fall down. Saltwater heals all wounds, the Mermother knows, even hurt feelings. But she also knows it cannot protect them, these innocents, from the anger of men who are fathers and the weakness of women who are mothers. The Mermother's den is a refuge for these four, but she is worried about the others – the ones who need rescue.

Soon she will have to return the children to land. But not yet. She is waiting for a sign that the folks on shore are brave enough to face an uncertain future without frightening or abandoning their children.

Right now, she does not see the signs.

Right now, the moon is on the wane.

The Mermother lifts a heavy crown from her head and plucks from it a pearl. It is the size of a small lantern, and it glows with the pulse of a living heart. She clicks her tongue once. A sleek dolphin, twice the size of any you've ever seen, swims forward and puts his head in her soft-scaled lap. The Mermother fastens the pearl around the dolphin's neck with a strand of seaweed and instructs him: Take this pearl into the heart of Coney Island. The heart lies where a mother's arms can't reach. It lies with the youngsters who have embraced the warmth most fervently.

In an instant, the dolphin is gone, swimming parallel to the shore across a trackless ocean and around the Point until he reaches the brackish creek that serves as a watery trash dump for Coney's castoffs. Navigating his way through the abandoned go-karts, rusted klieg lights and deflated beach balls of the marina, the dolphin finds the entrance to an underground spring feeding the canals of Luna Park. Emerging among the gondolas of Little Venice, the dolphin springs, as if shot from an underwater geyser, across the walkway of the central plaza and over a livery of pedicabs to land on the top of the water slide.

The plaza is empty – there is no one to witnesses the fantastic creature slaloming down the slide to plunge into the lagoon below. He does not resurface.

When the dolphin arrives at the Mermother's side some time later, the pearl is gone from his neck.

Well done, says the Mermother. She scratches the sleek creatures head and wraps her tail more snugly around the sleeping Mary Lou Walker. Well done.

CHAPTER ELEVEN

B uff rises late the next morning, startled awake by a dream he can't remember. From his bedroom window he can see the ocean and on it, a narrow, glinting ribbon unfurled.

Used to be, that shine meant wind.

Nowadays it's probably just a slick spot of dead fish.

Buff scrambles from bed and stretches. He puts on his swim trunks and trousers and stuffs a towel into his rucksack. He taps his chin, thinking of his plans with Paloma. He throws a flashlight and a Swiss-army knife into his bag, and then, remembering the silent Funny Faces from last night, he finds his sling-shot in the drawer with his socks. That goes in the bag as well.

Downstairs, in the snug kitchen looking over a modest vegetable garden, Buff pours milk into a bowl of cornflakes and hums along with the radio. He glances at the morning paper lying on the table as he eats. On the front page is a grainy photo of a ship, the name SS St Louis painted on its starboard flank. Above the photo, a headline reads: REFUGEE SHIP TURNED BACK TO EUROPE.

The clock strikes ten, distracting Buff from the news. But he wonders, as he pulls his shoes on hurriedly, why folks would be fleeing St. Louis. He's halfway down the front steps when he hears a familiar salutation behind him.

"I've got my eye on you."

"Morning, Doc," says Buff, turning to greet the old man sitting in a wind-worn rocking chair on the porch. Martin Couney is dressed in an immaculate white suit, as white as his bushy hair and side-whiskers, but his feet are bare and browned by the sun. Buff, who has lived with Doc ever since he emerged healthy but homeless from his miraculous hot-box, knows the old man's habits well. "I thought you'd be beachcombing by now."

"The sea is upset last night," says Doc. "I sink I shouldn't find nussink but sea-bile today."

Last night, when Buff arrived home all worked up about "thugs" and "miasmas," Doc had put a hand on the boy's forehead and delivered his diagnosis: "Miasma, yes. Terribly contagious, but easily cured." He prescribed a tall glass of Ovaltine and sent Buff off to bed. It had worked, but now the mention of "sea-bile" makes Buff's stomach recoil lightly, as if it, too, is churned up by something noxious.

"So. Where are you off to today?" asks Doc. "If you go looking for trouble..."

"I'm sure to find it," Buff finishes for him. "I know."

He bites his lip. It occurs to him that, for once, he is indeed out looking for trouble and hoping to find it. The idea makes him queasier, and for a moment he considers the comfort of his bed, the quiet of his story-booth, or the safety of Doc's kitchen. But these images are quickly replaced by another - a sea turtle, buried in the sand but vulnerable all the same. Without asking himself how he knows, Buff understands that he can't afford to stay out of trouble. Not anymore.

"No story-telling for you today?" Doc asks.

"I haven't had a customer in weeks," shrugs the boy.

Buff waits for Doc's response, another dismissal of the story-telling booth that had once seemed so promising. But Doc is silent.

"I know what you're thinking," prods Buff. "You were right. It was a dumb idea."

"Not dumb," replies Doc, shaking his snow-white head. "Not dumb. Just ..." He puts his foot down on the porch and ceases rocking. "You must remember dat Luna Park has a stronger claim on you zen on some menchen shopkeeper," he says. "It is, in some sense, your psychic birthplace. De Incubator House is for always and ever replaying vat we know as de 'natal trauma.' It is de nexus of new life and vatnot. Dat story booth is like burrowing into your birthplace."

Buff turns his eyes to the ground and kicks a pebble,

ping, against the step. "Ain't about psychology, Doc," he mutters. "I'm just looking for, you know, my calling. You've heard the fellas say it a million times: 'you're a born storyteller, Buff, that's what you are. Just a natural born storyteller.'"

Doc smiles. Buff is a good mimic of his carny peers.

"But dese are careless words, Buff. You, of everyone, should know a storyteller you were not born. You were born how? Mit no patience and worse odds. You were an overenthusiastic entry. A tiny too tiny man who had to be safe-keeped in a glass box or else run right out of his brand-new life – auf wiedersehen."

Doc pulls a white handkerchief from his sleeve and waves an imaginary goodbye.

"You have all ze time in ze world to decide for what you were born, my child. If it is for telling tales, zat is most excellent, indeed. But you must not be in a hurry."

But I am, thinks Buff. I'm in a terrible hurry.

Buff climbs the steps to the boardwalk and surveys the ocean. It looks placid enough, despite Doc's thoughts on sea-bile. He heads east toward the funparks and the piers. As he walks, he begins to remember snatches of the dream that had slid away on waking. He had dreamt of a ship—a merry sort of good-time cruise ship that churned up the water behind it like … well, like music. He hears an echo of the notes, jangling and tumbling as if from a player piano.

Hitching up his pants, he lets his feet dance to the old-fashioned music in his head.

Not a bad way to cross the water,
Buoyed up by some ragtime jazz.
Certainly beats swimming.

First the jelly-roll, then the maple leaf rag, propel Buff down the boardwalk. He's just started on a walking version of the Shreveport Stomp when he pulls up in front of Handsome Henry, who's watching with amusement.

"That's quite a soft-shoe you have there, Buff."

Buff just hums in reply. The player piano in his head has slowed to a more soulful rhythm, which he makes audible as he sits and pulls at his shoestrings.

"Oh you do, do you?" asks the bally-man.

Buff turns and raises an eyebrow.

"You have the St. Louis Blues? That's what that's called, that most spiritual of ragtime tunes."

Handsome Henry leans back and joins in with a surprisingly rich bass: "Hate to see the evening sun go down. 'Cause my baby done left town."

Buff stops his humming and says, "St. Louis, huh? Like the boat what got turned back.

Henry looks at the boy in surprise. "Matter of fact, yes. You read about that? Crying shame. Folks booted out of their homes and won't nobody give them refuge."

"Where are their homes?"

"Germany."

Germany. Just like Doc. Except Doc left his home. He didn't get chased from it.

It's something that Buff is reminded of a lot, lately. He remembers the day long ago, when he first learned that Doc Couney and Coney Island were not one and the same. He was just beginning to read, and as he was spelling out the name printed on the certificates lining Doc's office in the Incubator House, he wondered over that extra vowel.

"There's no U in Coney."

"To be sure there is a me in Coney," answered Doc, quick as a wink. "And a 'U' too."

And just like that, Buff learned that Doc Couney came from somewhere else. It was a surprise—for everything that made Coney Island what it was seemed to derive from Doc's Incubators. There was the sun, nature's own grow-lamp. There was the beach, holding onto the day's heat to warm the night. And there was the boardwalk, which clinked with nickels and dimes and pumped them through the park like a wide-planked heart.

Doc Couney worshipped the same God that Coney Island did—the one who saw a million Luna Park light bulbs illuminate the Brooklyn sky and said, "That's surepop sockola!"

But no, he had told the young boy trying tomake sense of C-O-U-N-E-Y. He was from the Old World, across the ocean.

Buff feels another small cramp in his stomach. He is thinking of the angry little man who Doc says will make it impossible for him to go home again. Hitler, says Doc is a "tyrant," but the newsreels call him something else — something boring and bureaucratic. "The Chancellor," that was it.

What kind of chancellor makes people flee their homes?

"So why couldn't they come here? Those people on the St. Louis?" Buff asks.

"Hard to say," Henry replies. "People, when they feel uneasy, tend to shut their doors."

"Clam up," adds Buff.

"That's right. That's how it is. The folks on the St. Louis are getting the worst end of it—bullies at home and cowards across the street. Or the ocean, if you will."

Buff sits still, his eyes on the gray horizon and his mind wrestling again with the lost dream. There had been a woman. On a ship. Holding a bundle. A baby. Her arms outstretched … but it was gone.

"Planning to swim this morning?"

Buff shudders, an involuntary answer.

"Sure I am," he says. But he makes no move.

"Want me to walk down to the water with you?" asks Henry after some time.

Buff shakes his head and in doing so, seems to shake off his reluctance. "Nope," he says, "I'm gonna make short work of it today, Handsome. I'll be out and back before you can finish the end of those blues."

Buff jumps from the bench and hops over the rail at the edge of the boardwalk. With his feet in the sand he strips off his shirt and pants and sprints for the water. Henry watches his young friend's awkward dash and thinks, not for the first time, that Buff is almost as challenged by land as he is by water.

As he watches the boy wade into the surf, Henry notices something out of the corner of his eye; a solitary freighter is headed towards the Point, churning the Atlantic behind its broad stern. The sight of the ship in his peripheral vision catches him the same instant as a sudden smell of rotten eggs. Henry considers the vessel for a moment. You don't normally see a freighter headed that direction, as if on course for Queens instead of open water, he thinks. His mind wanders to the other boat, the St. Louis. The one that had come all the way across the ocean only to be turned away. The one that was full of Germans. Germans who had been ruled 'not-German' because they were also Jews. Like Henry himself.

How many kids on that ship, he wonders.

How many mothers?

And then he thinks of the children closer to home – the ones who have been stolen from their mothers, right here in Brooklyn.

Well, at least they're all in it together out there on THE ST. LOUIS.

The bally-man settles his hat over his eyes to cut the glare. The thought of the ship full of families in search of safety won't leave him alone. It nags at him like a hungry seagull. Like the sulfurous smell of eggs. He shifts on the bench, leaning forward and then back and then sitting bolt upright. He can't get comfortable, but his discomfort isn't physical. It's somewhere else. It's with the ship and her unhappy passengers. Especially the mothers – the women who cannot save their children alone.

"Enough to make you ashamed to be an American," he mutters under his breath.

B uff skims the surface of the water with the tips of his fingers and thinks of creatures for whom the sea is a sanctuary. That's why she has so many babies, the sea-turtle mama - she knows that one of them has to make it.

His stomach constricts, and he touches the spot of the cramp. *Once,* he thinks, sliding a wet fingertip around the sensitive ridges of his belly-button, *I was connected to a mother.*

Was she sorry to leave me?

Or did she know?

That life is a game of chance?

And I was a bad bet.

Buff turns and looks back to the boardwalk where Henry is no more than a shape against the weathered stripes of the summer's awnings and shadows.

As long as he can see me, he thinks, I'll be okay.

Buff fills his lungs with an exaggerated gasp and dives headfirst into the water. He moves his arms and legs, commanding his mind to be quiet while he negotiates the mechanics of hydromotion. But his thoughts twitter with measurements, growing louder and bossier. A fresh cramp forces Buff to abandon his sidestroke, to stop breathing, to open his eyes and see how far he's come and divide that by how far he's gone and...

Buff inhales at the wrong moment, sucking seawater. He splutters and chokes and reaches a toe for the bottom, but he is out over his head and his foot finds no floor. He works his limbs faster, still coughing, and tries to see beyond the tears in his eyes. Water nips his ears and then rushes in, filling them eagerly. Buff cries out in alarm at the change in tune, and now he is sinking, swallowing another mouthful of sea. His brain has gone quiet, silenced by fear, leaving his body, finally, in charge. But it's too late. His feet are dead weight; his arms as disembodied as a jellyfish's severed tentacle. He is in panic. Twisting, Buff raises his face to the sky and tries to lie on his back.

Float like a dead man and you are sure to stay alive, is what Handsome always says. But the waves refuse to stay flat and Buff finds himself falling like a boy out of bed. He claws his way up once more, this time facing the shore, which swims as woozily as the open sea.

"Henry!" Buff calls, just as another wave tucks him under its cover.

From his lookout on the boardwalk bench, Handsome Henry peers out from under the brim of his hat at the sun's brief glare. He wonders if it's too much to hope for, a day that is as sunny as it is not. Buff is about a third of the way to the buoy when the sun drops behind the clouds.

Henry scans the horizon and finds the freighter as it disappears around the Point. He smells again the soft stench and decides it's the ship that is to blame, though he knows it doesn't stand to reason.

He watches Buff make slow progress and smiles at the boy's persistence. Henry's lids are heavy. His coffee, cold.

Underwater there is a sandstorm. A sandstorm split through with a cyclone of bubbles, and Buff, thrashing, is its vortex.

He struggles, certain that he won't emerge alive. But

then, in the chaos of drowning, a watery curtain parts and reveals an audience of wide-eyed suckerfish watching his flailing with interest.

Buff stops thrashing, and the water stills. He peers into the becalmed darkness and his heart skips a beat. Because the eight eyes gazing back at him are not the eyes of fish at all. The faces ripple like a mirage in the flat water, but Buff is certain they are real. Real enough to touch him. Real enough to save him. He's not surprised that among them is a girl, the same girl he saw yesterday...when he was not underwater...and when she was already missing.

A dark shadow passes over Buff's head. He looks up and recognizes a spinning gyre slicing through the water – a miniature Wonder Wheel come unmoored from the boardwalk. Distracted by the spinning toy, the four faces turn to chase the wheel through gentle waves.

Buff reaches out both hands: take me with you. But they are gone, riding away on slow-moving carousel horses. Something glints in the darkness of their distance. Buff knows what it is: the brass ring. The brass ring that pulls every carousel rider sideways in a lunge for glory. Buff pushes forward to follow the riders and seize the ring, but the curtain closes before him and he is blind. He sees nothing more until tumbled, tossed, somersaulted and sanded, he sees the light of day.

Henry starts from his drowsiness to see a lone wave draw a steep line across the horizon. He stands, surprised at the sudden whitecap. He can't see Buff. And then he can. He covers his mouth, stifling a half-laugh, half-gasp, as Buff, Coney Island's weakest swimmer, surfs a rogue wave to shore with a rare swagger.

Buff opens his eyes. Weak and bruised, he retches seawater from his gut and wipes sand from his mouth. There is a warm hand on his shoulder and Henry squats beside him, his mouth moving. Buff can't hear what he is saying; the sea still has her hands clapped soundly over his ears. He watches Henry talk, recognizing the same calm assurance that he shows when the roller-coaster next door to the bally-stage drowns out his spiel with train full of screams.

The boy closes his burning eyes and watches a line of sea turtles swim across the backs of his eyelids. With them swim every sliver of his underwater discovery. In a split second the vision fades from revelation to confusion to … gone.

He has forgotten what he saw when he very nearly drowned.

Almost.

Oh. I saw it happen…

Goodbye Coney Island, and good riddance…

Late again, story-boy?

That's quite a softshoe, Buff…

They're HERE. They're REAL. They're ALIVE!

Sweet Shirley Temple!

CHAPTER TWELVE

Mingus Lamont is perched on top of an old fireworks crate in a cramped, makeshift shed that rattles violently to the rhythm of the nearby Thunderbolt roller coaster. A gang of boys slouch before him, each one a bigger disappointment to his mother than the last. All of them hold a cheap Funny Face mask tied at the back with string.

"The heck am I supposed to do with this?" one of the goons asks.

"You cover yer ugly mug with it, that's what you do."

Seeing a lack of cooperation on the boy's real face, the manager of Steeplechase Park snaps, "You wanna wear yer own face you can, Bugs. But since you skipped probation last weekend, the only thing that'll get you is a trip back to the slammer. Suit yourself."

Lamont is instructing his crew, ten bad apples ranging from age fourteen to nineteen, in a new "procedure." One that he is working the kinks out of, but will be implemented any day now.

"Half the kids who come into this joint every day are just misfits anyway," he is explaining. "Runaways, maybe. Or mopers. Some of 'em might come down to Coney with the express purpose of making trouble. Or a stink, you know? A mountain in a haystack. A teapot in a storm. They're just looking for you know, attention."

At this point Lamont holds his hands up to his ears, palms to the heavens, in a sign of utter lack of understanding for the perverse behavior of kids these days.

"So what we're gonna do is we're gonna keep 'em outta trouble ... deliver them into safe hands. Take 'em where they can get a fresh start – and I don't mean the junior joint where no-goods like you get sent. No, this is a real sweetheart deal. They get a free ride to the World's Fair."

Mingus Lamont jumps down from his perch and eyes his crew. He sticks his thumbs into dirty suspenders and rocks back on his heels. Next to him, a muscular bruiser pulls a bowie knife from his boot and starts picking his teeth with the point.

"And what happens then, Ming?" he asks. "You gonna give 'em a pair of roller skates and a silver dollar?"

Mingus Lamont moves fast as a snake. A moment later the knife is sticking straight up in the toe of the boy's heavy boot. The boy, whose name is Jinx, stares wide-eyed at his newly accessorized footwear.

"What happens then, you dumb lummox, is they get rescued, they get their picture in the paper, and everybody lives happily ever after," hisses Lamont. "That's the plan.

Now keep that mask on and a sharp eye out. And remember what I said: ya don't get anywhere in the freight and delivery business if you don't stick together, avoid the unions and keep yer gob shut. Otherwise it's back to the joint I sprung youse from."

Lamont glares at his crew, trying to underscore his authority with a hard eye. But his left eye grows distracted and wanders away, so the nasty little carny resorts to Latin for emphasis: "Habeas corpus and de facto el presto," he announces in a voice that dares someone to argue.

"Right-o, Mr. Lamont," says Jinx.

Mingus Lamont straightens his stooped shoulders and crosses the small room to stand before a hand-drawn chart hanging on the wall. The chart has three columns, each one a messy array of numbers and letters that looks more like a code than the schedule it's meant to be.

"This'll be a quick turnaround job," he says as he pulls the cap from the thick marker hanging by a string next to the chart. "Kids don't have much of a shelf-life for storage, dontcha know. But we aim for delivery in two weeks time." He makes a notation on the chart and takes a step back to consider his work. Then he writes one last notation in big block letters directly on the plywood door and raps it solidly with his knuckle.

TURN OUT DA LIGHT, reads one of the better-schooled ruffians.

"Dis is all on the low-down," hisses Lamont. "Breathe a word about it to anyone and I knock yer block off."

Then, without another glance at his minions, the manager of Steeplechase Park exits the cramped shed, muttering to himself that he knows where the future is brightest. And it sure ain't in the la-la land of Coney Island.

Buff stands shakily from the sand and lets Handsome Henry lead him back to the boardwalk. He doesn't talk, but he doesn't need to. Henry is busy giving his account of the splendid spectacle that was Buff mastering the surf, riding the tide like Neptune himself.

"No wonder your knees are wobbly, kid. You musta been kissed by a mermaid to be riding that high!"

Buff listens to his friend bluster. His pale face stays blank. He knows for certain that his deposit on shore was not the heroic feat Henry is describing. But he can't decide what else he knows for sure. Underneath his scraped skin and bruised ego is the lingering feeling that something else entirely had happened out of Henry's view. He glances up at his friend and wonders, for the first time, if maybe Handsome Henry, the sharp-eyed bally-man, had not noticed.

When they reach the boardwalk Buff puts his shirt on backwards and his shoes on the wrong feet. He licks his lips and tastes salt. It reminds him of tears, not of the sea.

"Henry?" he asks.

"Yeah, kid."

"What's down there?"

"Down where?"

"Under the buoy. At the end of the pier. What is it that sunk in the fire and never came up?"

Henry removes his hat and scratches his head.

"There was a carousel on the pier. A real beaut' — with hand-painted stallions and gold gilt carriages. They rescued a few of the horses, but the carousel itself, the gazebo – it was never retrieved."

Henry turns to look back at the ocean. "It was before my time," he continues. "Long before I came to Coney. The Dreamland fire. They say the smoke took a week to clear, and who knows what got lost in the ruins – lifted and carted off with or without the help of the flames. I've heard tell that there was a miniature stargazing theater on the pier as well. An observatory they call it. Now that's something to mourn. Imagine — a place where you could see the old man in the moon close enough to poke him in the eye."

Henry chuckles and smoothes his mustache thoughtfully. "The rest of it, well ... what Coney loses, Coney finds. All the dreams of Dreamland – they found another day and another dollar."

Buff follows Henry's gaze out to the buoy-bell that

marks the end of the ruined pier. The pylons, weathered and smooth, are like teeth in a wide, watery mouth. Buff is used to imagining the wonders that once floated above the water, supported by the stumps. Now he is curious to see what lies beneath.

"How come no one ever looked down there?" he asks, half to himself.

"Who says they haven't? Like I said, what Coney loses, Coney finds. One man's loss is another man's treasure. If that old observatory hasn't come apart in the waves, Buff, well, heck. It could be yours for the looting – just as soon as you learn to hold your breath a bit longer."

Henry is smiling, but Buff's face is serious. He is turning the bally-man's words over in his mind:

What Coney loses, Coney finds.

Except for the things that are lost forever.

As if on cue, the Funny Face blares its catch-phrase from the Pavilion of Fun: "Looka, looka, looka!"

I will, Buff thinks. I will.

Officer Ramsey is staring glumly at the small notebook that contains the sum total of his investigation over the past few weeks. Page after page of nonsensical notes taunt him, mocking his attempt to answer a simple question – what happened out there?

He was right there, tugging at the back of my skirt...

When I went back to find them, our umbrella was gone and the sand castle had sunk...

He disappeared during lunch. I know because the moon was directly overhead...

I saw him go. He walked right into its shadows...

Ramsey frowns.

What shadow? he wonders. The testimonies read like riddles. But why hadn't he tried to make sense of them? Why hadn't he pressed the mother of the last one, Mary Lou Walker, when she told him "We'll leave the light on for her, but they'll just shut it off again."

And now, to crown the gibberish clues, he has just added another: the ghost ship, MIASMA.

"Good grief," he sighs, throwing the pencil down in aggravation.

This was new information that came from that gadfly, Clyde. A boat, said Clyde, who was up before dawn fishing for bream, had docked at the Steeplechase pier in the dark and pulled out close to sunrise.

"She was about the size of a tug but with a deep cargo hold. Saw one or two lads pushing a loading cart full of boxes up to the hold. But other than that it coulda been a ghost ship for all the trace it left. In and out in less time than I could bait my line and never did see a captain."

"Did it have a registration number? A name?" asked Ramsey.

"No number. But looked to me like her name was MIASMA."

"Miasma? Whatsit — a foreign boat?"

But then Clyde had gotten the telephone cord tangled in fishing line and the conversation had ended.

Officer Ramsey pulls a handkerchief from his breast pocket and wipes his clammy neck. His calls to the local marinas have come up empty - there are no records of a boat called the Miasma. Worse, his calls to Police Headquarters have gone unanswered.

"You'd think I was the sheriff of a one-horse town, not the guy in charge of public safety for all of South Brooklyn!" he exploded, slamming down the phone on an unconcerned dispatcher from One Police Plaza.

Officer Ramsey is mad. He's mad because he has run the Coney Island precinct for close to seven years, and now he feels like a rookie. He's busted up bootleggers, cuffed convicts and hauled more than one gangster into court, but he's spent the last two weeks acting like an amateur. Armed robbery, unlawful trespassing and public disorder are Ramsey's bread and butter, but now he's stumped by a handful of kids gone missing. And that makes him mad. That's what he tells himself, at least: mad as hell! Because as long as he's mad, he doesn't have to be scared.

"Nothing to be scared of," he mutters. But the thought of failure – of more children disappearing and taking his job with them – haunts him. So does the memory of Lionel Bangs turning his face away from the policeman's frustration. And so do the words spoken by Buff yesterday morning: "Maybe you saw it too? "

"Nothing to be scared of," he mumbles again. He bends down and slowly opens the bottom drawer of his desk. There lies the ragdoll, her button eyes blazing with accusation. He slams the drawer shut quickly.

Officer Sherman Ramsey, a grown man, fights the urge to stick his thumb in his mouth and crawl under the desk.

CHAPTER THIRTEEN

Handsome Henry was right – the Dreamland fire of 1911 was a short-lived disaster. The ashes had barely cooled when the first impresarios showed up on Surf Avenue, eager to stake their claim in the drifting smoke. These showmen's fantastical attractions: **VESUVIUS FROZEN IN TIME** (brought to you by the world-famous Italian scholar Lorenzo Fabreezy); **JOURNEY ACROSS MONGOLIA** (featuring the world's only convoy of triple-humped dromedaries); and **THE FEATS OF HERCULES** (starring the Macedonian monster himself), just to name a few – were Coney Island's biggest draw for more than a decade. But the greatest of the great Surf Avenue Theatrical Spectaculars was also the last: **STOCK MARKET CRASH** was a short spectacle, not more then fifteen minutes long, but the crowds lined up daily to see brick banks reduced to rubble, top-hatted millionaires stripped to their skivvies, and – the moment they had all been waiting for – wheelbarrows full of bright green currency burned in a climactic bonfire.

And then it was over.

Because after the Crash came the Depression. Money was worthless and jobs were scarce. Nobody had the dough to front a box-office, let alone burn on stage. The years of Depression proved much harder to recover from than a one-night fire, and so, that once-bustling stretch of Surf Avenue lay low, its grand theatre foyers chopped up into humble enterprises: a dank-smelling pet store that carries mostly reptiles; a photography studio that opens on whim; and, on the mezzanine level of the Oceanic Opera House, a narrow alcove with a worn blue carpet for a door and a sign that reads **MADAME FORTUNA: PROPHECY PARLOR.**

It is here that Mingus Lamont, his eyes still adjusting to the dim of a low-watt crystal ball in a windowless room, is trying to make a business deal.

"Lemme explain this for you one more time, Rita," he whines. "These disappearances, they don't have to be a tragedy, see. You just gotta know how to make the best of a sad situation. You know – lemons into lemonade and all that."

Across a small, round table from him, a woman wearing heavy makeup and heavier gold jewelry regards the carny impassively as she spreads a spoonful of whitefish salad on a bagel. The long red nails of Rita Chervinsky, aka Madame Fortuna, click maddeningly against the table as Mingus Lamont watches her chew.

"Look into yer crystal ball then if that's what ya gotta

do, but I'm tellin' ya, Rita – you ain't gonna find a surer bet than the picture I'm paintin' for ya right now."

The woman pops the last of her breakfast into her mouth. She wipes her hand on the skirt of the table and smoothes her short hair into a net in preparation for the elaborate headdress that will transform her into Madame Fortuna, visionary and psychic.

"Let me get this straight," she says in a voice distinctly free of its business-hours gypsy flavor. "You want me to hypnotize a bunch of kids in order to keep them from getting seasick? That's the nuttiest thing I ever heard."

"But you can do it, can't you Rita? You can, you know, put 'em in a trance? Cast a spell or somethin'? So they don't remember nothin about how they got where they're going and who took em' there. Right? That's easy for a lady with your … er…talents."

"Look, Mingus," says Rita. "I can do anything for two hundred bucks. I can put YOU in a trance so deep you'll forget what a weasel you are. But what I want to know is – who the heck would ask for such a loony birthday party, huh?"

Mingus Lamont, who is neither a patient nor a smart man, feels frustration mounting as he regards this fortuneteller with no entrepreneurial vision. He considers lying and regrets, briefly, that he doesn't have a decent lie prepared. He throws his hat on the floor and stomps on it, once. Then he puts his smashed hat back on his head, leans across the table and pronounces in a conspiratorial whisper: "This comes all the way from the Commissioner. Play along and you might get to move out of this flea-bit closet. Decline, and don't be surprised if you get shut down at the end of the season."

At that, Rita Chervinsky, a double divorcee who lost all her savings at the age of sixty-five during the stock market crash, leans back in her chair and says, "Show me the money."

A cool breeze greets Officer Ramsey at the top of the boardwalk stairs, and he pauses to relish it. Closing his eyes, he conjures up the memory of summer afternoons full of endless sunshine, pale blue skies, and a sea of colorful beach umbrellas. Summer afternoons when nothing disappears except maybe the afternoon itself. He listens to the languid flap of the boardwalk flags and tries to pretend it's the chatter of hundreds of weekenders on their day off. But when he opens his eyes he can hardly see the shoreline. To his right the Wonder Wheel is cloaked in an inhospitable haze. The breeze is gone and the boardwalk is lonesome.

The cop squints at an approaching figure - Mingus Lamont is darting through the soupy air. They are practically nose to nose when the stooped carny notices the cop.

He pulls up short and gives a surprised snort.

"Mingus Lamont," says Ramsey by way of greeting, "whaddya know?"

"Not a thing, Officer," answers Lamont quickly, shrugging his shoulders to his ears. "I don't know a thing and, in fact, I'm completely in the dark."

Ramsey cocks an eyebrow and leans closer to the little man's flushed face.

"So you can't tell me anything about the cargo boat that docked up at the Steeplechase Pier early this morning?"

"Absolutely not, no sir. Haven't seen or heard of such a thing." Lamont tries and fails to look Ramsey in the eye. His own are scuttling in opposite directions. "But I did read in the papers about how there are all kinds of boats pullin' into New York harbor these days, or at least, trying to pull in. On accounta the trouble over in Europe..." Lamont fails to suppress a snide snicker. "Maybe I oughta send some of my manpower to help them, er ...reroute their cargo."

Ramsey leans closer and says, "You know what I think? I think you'd be smart to keep your resources close to home, Mingus. I wouldn't want you to come up short."

A crooked smile wavers on Mingus Lamont's face and then disappears as fast as a coin in Madame Fortuna's palm.

"Watch who you're calling 'short,' Ramsey," he hisses. "Looks can be deceiving down here on Coney Island."

And with that, the slighted Steeplechase boss continues on his way down the boardwalk.

Ramsey watches him go, stewing over his parting words. He's right, he thinks, looks can be deceiving. Hell, all of Coney Island is built on optical illusions. I saw him go…he walked right into the shadow of the moon.

"Doesn't make a lick of sense," he says out loud.

"What's that, Ramsey?" asks a voice over his shoulder. The policeman turns to find the Sideshow barker, Handsome Henry.

"None of it. It don't none of it make any sense. I had a call this morning from a lady says she found a Funny Face in her melon patch and Clyde telling me there's a ghost ship docked at Steeplechase."

"Ghost ship, huh?"

"Yeah and it weren't the Half Moon from Greta's Sea Geekery if that's what your gonna tell me. It was a boat called the Miasma."

Henry shifts on his feet and looks back over his shoulder to the stretch of boardwalk where earlier he had smelled an unhealthy odor and spied a strange ship. To where he had just left Buff with a chuck on the shoulder and some meaningless words of encouragement. A shudder of concern runs up his spine.

"Miasma, huh?" he murmurs, lifting his bowler and settling it back on his head.

"Yep. And I got testimonies even more slippery. Fuzzy notions of what folks saw, or think they saw, or think they think they saw. I can't get a reliable witness any more than I can get a qualified detective to back me up."

"People think they see all kinds of things down here," agrees Handsome Henry. "Sometimes it's real. The dime someone dropped on the tracks of a dark ride, say, shining clear as day. Doesn't mean you can reach it, though. And sometimes folks see something that they can all agree on, but can't agree what it means. Sort of like Groundhog's Day. We all agree that the thing saw its shadow or didn't see its shadow, but then we argue whether it means that its gonna get darker or that there's light at the end of the tunnel."

A young girl on roller skates passes appears on the boardwalk. Henry and Ramsey, alert, follow her with their eyes through the haze. They aren't the only ones – leaning up against the Pavilion of Fun are two fellas with sinewy arms under short sleeves and faces masked by the leering Funny Face.

Henry and Ramsey exchange a glance.

Just then, the skater trips over a popped boardwalk plank and dives headfirst into a garbage bin. The Funny Faces bark in laughter. Henry is about to rush to her assistance when the girl rights herself, throws back her shoulders, flips her thumb under her bloodied chin at the laughing boys and pushes off on her wheeled way.Henry and Ramsey watch the masked youths disappear down the ramp to the Pavilion of Fun.

"Shady characters, them," says the cop.

"Yep," agrees Henry. "Pair of pretty unpromising groundhogs, those two." He tugs at his mustache and remembers the girl's defiance. He remembers Buff's pale resolve.

"I'm still inclined to bet on the light," he says.

But when he parts with Ramsey, the bally-man begins to make plans. Handsome Henry has seen too many bets gone bad and too many lights put out.

CHAPTER FOURTEEN

Buff is halfway down the Bowery when he notices the silence. It's not the Bowery itself that's quiet. Even at this hour, the stretch of saloons and dance halls clangs with the tired whoops and insults that follow a devil-may-care night. Two rats squabble over a corncob and a handful of rough customers shoot dice in an alley. Buff hears all these sounds, but his head is quiet.

Not a hint of a tune, not a whisper of melody. There is no song in his ears.

Buff shakes his head slowly, as if to dislodge a few notes from a hiding spot. He jumps on one foot and knocks his temple, but only a trickle of seawater emerges. He touches his elbow where Henry's strong hands had pulled him to his feet from the sand. The skin is tender and chafed. His knees, too, are rubbed raw. He flinches at the burn, then hurries the rest of the way up the Bowery to Bettleman's Dancehall and hollers.

"Paloooooooma."

She appears in the second-story window, pulls a face at Buff, and disappears again. Now the side door slams shut and Paloma skitters down the stairs into the street.

"What took you so long?" she asks but she doesn't wait for an answer. Instead she rolls up her dungarees, declares that there's work to be done and marches up the Bowery towards Steeplechase Park. As Buff hurries to keep up, the last bit of the Atlantic Ocean drains from his ear.

On a good day, each of the mechanical horses on Steeplechase's signature ride would carry two racers, clinging to each other in delight as they careered towards the finish line of Steeplechase Park's favorite attraction. Today there is exactly one rider on the entire circuit.

A flat-faced kid is rounding the bend alone, bereft of competition. He holds the reins morosely. His horse has a paint-flecked mane and a static grimace of cracked teeth. It slows to a standstill some fifty feet from the end of the ride. The stranded rider kicks and complains, but the horse goes nowhere. Buff and Paloma are watching his frustration.

"That Mingus Lamont sure hasn't done Steeplechase any favors," observes Paloma.

Buff nods. The silence hurts his ears. "No music," he notes. "How about that? He's got rid of the music."

"Lamont's the Commissioner's toady," replies Paloma. "He'd asphalt the beach if that was orders."

"The clowns are all gone, too."

"I think they've been replaced."

Paloma jerks her head towards the operator making his way along the track towards the marooned rider. He's wearing a Funny Face mask.

"They're everywhere," says Buff scanning the park. Sure enough, another half-dozen masked figures can be seen positioned along the perimeter of the park. Buff and Paloma are quiet. They feel the menace, but not like yesterday. In the sleepy mid-morning, the Funny Faces just look bored. And about as helpful as a barbed wire fence. Buff watches as a little boy, focused on the cheap yo-yo he has gotten tangled in its string, runs smack into one of the masked youths. The little boy looks up into the maniacal mask, bursts into startled tears, and runs for his mother.

Buff watches her wipe away his tears and frown at the slouching Funny Face, before herding the child towards the exit.

"Let's go check out the Pavilion of Fun," he says, wondering if there could possibly be any fun left.

Inside the enormous vaulted building that runs the length of Steeplechase's boardwalk property, the children thread their way through the Down & Out Tube, the Hootenanny and the Tilted Windmill. The rides that aren't completely deserted have a forlorn air, nevertheless. The people emerging from them seem more harassed than entertained. A Funny Face is fishing pennies from the kiddy boat ride.

Paloma, in spite of herself, is eyeing the Human Niagara, her favorite ride in the Pavilion. "How about just once, Buff?" she asks. "There's no line at all."

But Buff isn't listening. She glances at him and recognizes that faraway look he gets when he has finished telling a story that doesn't end quite right. His lips are moving, but Paloma can't hear him over the din of the flying bicycles, which are in need of a good oiling.

Buff, still struggling to understand what happened in the surf this morning, has started to recall more of the dream he had in the night. There was another ship besides the St. Louis –a ship that sailed over a giant waterfall. And on it, too, there were mothers in distress. And there was a ship hauling light and a ship hauling darkness ... and a ship that went up in flames.

Ashes, ashes, he whispers, seeing snatches of destruction, and then louder: "I had a very strange dream last night."

"Let's hear it," says Paloma.

Buff tries to weave the threads of dream – ships, fires, round and round –into a proper narrative, but it makes no sense.

Paloma scrunches up her nose and concludes: "So Coney's got another fire coming. That's nothing new.

Even Madame Fortuna doesn't bother with that forecast. And the ships? I'll bet you dreamed that up 'cause of Greta. Remember what she said? Something about a ship from Miami?"

Buff nods. "Not Miami. Miasma."

"Right. The loony ship."

On the other side of the Pavilion, Mingus Lamont is brandishing a broom and bad words. "Clear out ya miserable mutt or I'll turn you into hot dogs," he yells. He's chasing a stray dog that is gulping down a stolen wiener, all hunger and guilt. Buff knows Paloma will rush to the stray's rescue if he doesn't get them out of there quick. Spying a side-door, he pulls her away.

"Come on, Paloma, we're looking for clues, right?"

"Right."

Back outside, the children cross the park and climb through a hole in the fence. They find themselves in a weedy lot, on the far side of which the Thunderbolt roller coaster casts a long shadow.

"This place is so stripped down there's nowhere to hide anything anymore," Buff says. He turns in a circle, taking in the worn-out whimsy. It all seems particularly fragile in the murky sunlight. His eyes fall on a large dilapidated plywood building huddled up against the boardwalk under the Thunderbolt. Paloma has seen it too and now they are both scrambling under another halfhearted wire fence and over a pile of rubble to reach the door, which stands narrowly ajar. Squeezing through the gap, they find themselves in the Steeplechase warehouse, surrounded by the forgotten. Paloma climbs up on a long railing that runs along the inside wall and flings open several shuttered windows, startling pigeons with a flood of daylight.

The mix of mildew and dust gives Buff a sneezing fit. When it's over, his eyes fall on a giant figure standing in the slanting light of the open windows. He starts, and then recognizes the cutout that used to stand in the photo booth at the park entrance. He remembers the day that he talked Doc into posing in the cutout – becoming a benevolent Frankenstein's monster with white whiskers and a silly smile. Buff kept the snapshot by his bed for years, until it curled up into a worm and slipped behind the headstand. He feels a bit uneasy now, looking at the faceless monster. Knowing that there is no one watching you, or watching over you, he thinks, is as unsettling as the sensation of being watched.

"Hey, can I put these in your bag?" asks Paloma, tripping up behind him. She is wearing several strands of Mardi Gras beads and a tattered sailor's cap, and her arms are full of geegaws. "There's a whole trunk full of trick gyroscopes over there," she says. "And the turnstiles from the luau pit. Remember them? They moved

RING AROUND THE LUNA

up and down like a limbo stick."

"Pack rats make lousy detectives, Paloma," says Buff.

"Evidence," she protests.

Buff lifts the rusted door of a miniature jalopy with his toe. He thinks he remembers it from the kiddy rides but then wonders if he has only seen it in postcards.

So much of Coney's memories are memories of memories.Souvenirs of snapshots.

A past we never saw with our own eyes.

He wanders deeper into the musty dimness, looking for clues from today.

Or, at least, from yesterday.

Even yesterday seems long ago.

For a minute, Buff wonders why he hasn't told Paloma about his vision of Mary Lou Walker, the missing girl. She'd have a logical explanation, he thinks. Just like she did about the dream. But he knows that logic didn't make Mary Lou vanish. He tries to visualize the girl again, but her face has gone blurry, her features blurred as if underwater.

It occurs to Buff that they really should be down at the Wonder Wheel, where the girl was reported missing. Better yet, on the very top of the Wheel, with its full 360 degree view – a true ring around Luna.

Too bad it's busted, he thinks. The Wonder Wheel hasn't run since Memorial Day, when someone made off with metal doors on half the gondolas and nearly all the light bulbs that lit up the letters spelling **W-O-N-D-E-R**.

"Hey, Buff. I found somebody's clubhouse."

Buff makes his way across a littered terrain to find Paloma sitting proudly on a chariot, the remnant of some yesteryear parade. Behind her is a makeshift shed, a building within the building. A papier-mâché crocodile guards the small structure, albeit with a head that lolls at an unferocious angle.

Buff cautiously opens the door of the shed and steps inside. It is pitch dark and smells of unwashed boys. He takes another step and jumps at the touch of something on his cheek. Reaching up, he grasps the end of a string and pulls. The small room springs into the glare of a single naked bulb. On the wall facing the door someone has drawn a crude but instantly recognizable face – the Steeplechase Funny Face, only without the artistic details that give it its famous flair. Instead, the face is trapped in a bull's eye and pocked with holes. Someone has been using it for target practice.

Paloma follows Buff into the room and closes the door. Spying the chart on the wall, she moves closer to study it.

"A schedule," she says. Together they puzzle over the code scrawled across the heavy gridlines. The first line reads 5150120 LOWTROLLEYTRACK. The next, 610725 SODPLEXISTEEL. Six more entries brought the schedule to 626200 PEA0650 WIND.

Buff reads out loud: "Sixty two sixty two oh oh peas?" Each line has a thick black check mark next to it. Except for the final one, which is written in red ink and doesn't have a checkmark. It reads 742DOZBRATS2030HIGH.

Stamped in the corner of the chart in block letters is a single word: MIASMA.

The children are silent for a long time. Buff leans back against a stack of boxes, knocking one to the ground. It spills hundreds of small snaky tubes onto the floor. Buff picks one up. A Chinese finger cuff, a consolation prize that carnies give to kids who can't swing the hammer hard enough or throw the ball straight enough to win a real prize. You put a finger in either end of the tube and then you can't get them out. You are left a silly captive of your own making.

"Seven-forty-two. A dozen brats," he mumbles, twisting the cuff into a knot.

"Miasma," says Paloma.

They look at each other but don't speak. They have definitely found a clue, but neither of them feels pleased.

"I think we should go," says Paloma.

They scramble for the door and see its angry message:
TURN OUT DA LIGHT.

Buff feels a knot in his stomach.

Maybe the famously stingy Mingus Lamont is just conserving light bulbs, he reasons. But something tells him that the Steeplechase manager plans to purge the park of all its delight. And that he has some nasty goons and a vaporous boat to help him do it.

CHAPTER FIFTEEN

Handsome Henry is pacing the back lot of the Seashore Circus Sideshow. His mood has taken a dramatic dive since the morning and he can't get the smell of sulphur from his nose. He frowns deeply, wanting to be anywhere else but here. "Stick tight," he says through gritted teeth, "bet on the light."

Angelica DeMicco, known on stage as the Flame Eating Totem, watches Henry from a nearby picnic table. She sees him grab one of her unlit torches and raise it aloft.

"Fire," he says. "An eternal flame. A smoke signal."

In his other hand, Henry is using his showman's cane to sketch an elaborate blueprint in the dirt. He pauses to examine his work.

"We need to make a stand," he says decisively. "And we need to make a trap."

Angelica peels an orange and throws a section to Yums, the white terrier sitting alertly at her feet. Covered from head to toe in tattoos, Angelica is greeted with gasps of amazement in the dim mystery of the Sideshow, where she summons all of Coney's infernos and swallows them effortlessly. But here in the dusty daylight of the back lot, with her little dog and her canister of kerosene, the Flame Eating Totem looks more like the girl next door – Coney Island's own Dorothy Gale, fallen from Kansas into a bizarre land.

And Henry, she is thinking, is acting as peculiar as a two-bit phony wizard.

"Fire's risky business on the boardwalk, Handsome," she says. "You wanna help Officer Ramsey, you oughta just sit tight and keep an eye out."

Henry's rarely riled, so his sneer surprises her.

"Oh, sure. Watch and wait. Like they all do. Steal a peek and then pretend not to see. That's what's happening here."

Angelica pops another section of orange into her mouth and shrugs. "Speak for yourself, Handsome. Me? I ain't seen nothing out of the ordinary. That don't mean I'm gonna burn the place down looking."

"You're blinded," Henry replies. There's spite in his voice and spittle in his mustache. "It's what happens when you spend too much time in that circus tent. Too much time looking at one bright flame in the darkness. You need to get out and open your eyes. And you need to be ready to act."

Angelica scoops Yums onto her lap, and pats him on the head. "Oh, I'm ready, don't you worry. After all, Handsome, between you and me, I think we know which of us has more fire in the belly." She grins at her joke and her painted profile grins with her. "But for now, we got a show to put on."

The fire-eater nods towards the platform waiting in the front of the Sideshow. "Time to bally-hoo, Handsome. You got a job right here. Don't abandon your post to go chasing dragons."

With that, Angelica the Flame Eating Totem ducks into the tent. She is completely unaware that her words have hit a nerve with Henry, a man who knows something about abandonment and has never forgiven himself for it.

On the corner of Stillwell and Surf Avenues Buff is puzzling over the coded chart of the Miasma.

"When did the first kid go missing?" he asks and then answers his own question:

"Right around the time Mingus Lamont showed up."

"It was the weekend after opening day," adds Paloma. "Which, as I recall, was also the day Henry arrived for the season. Remember? How we asked him what kept him and how he said 'family affairs' and how mad he got when somebody made that crack about Handsome being about as much of a family man as Cheeks is the Lone Ranger?"

"What does Henry have to do with it?" Buff says. He slows his pace, but Paloma doesn't. She and her suspicions are getting further away by the second. "Why you gotta bring him into it?" he yells after her. "He's got nothing to do with it!"

Buff puts one hand on his elbow, rubbed raw from the sand of his morning crash with the beach. He sees, again, Henry's face over his, his mouth making words unheard.

"Henry's got nothing to do with it!" he says again. "Why would you even say that? I was talking about Mingus Lamont, the Steeplechase manager!"

Paloma turns and looks at her friend. But she doesn't see his pain, only confusion. So she explains: "Because Handsome and the hunchback are both carnies. They are 'Impresarios', Buff. Their job is to impress. And ain't nobody impressed with Coney Island no more, you can see for yourself. Desperate times call for desperate measures."

Buff shakes his head, a raucous noise like too many instruments warming up at once.

"Think about it, Buff," Paloma persists. "You're a carny. Your job is to create a spectacle. Something nobody thought possible. Something beyond our wildest dreams... something we don't know we want till they offer to sell it."

"Something you didn't know was missing till it was gone," says Buff softly.

"Exactly. What's a bally-man anyway? A man who speaks bally-hoo. The language of *follow me, I got something to show you*."

Paloma launches into a full-throated imitation of a sideshow barker: "Step right up! Greatest show on earth! Coney Island! Full of surprises and magic! Where one minute you're with mom and the next ... your gone!"

Buff opens his mouth to protest, but he's interrupted by the bally-man himself.

"They're HERE! They're REAL! They're ALIVE! Ladies and gentleman, boys and girls – they are ready to take the stage, our freaks of nature and self-made geeks! Ten acts. One ticket. Just a nickel for a kid and two nickels for the child at heart. Ten amazing specimen in one unforgettable show!"

Buff and Paloma turn the corner onto Cantilever Walk, where a small cluster of people has gathered outside the tents of the Seashore Circus Sideshow. Henry has begun his bally-hoo. He is dancing across the small platform in his peg-legged trousers and calico vest, his cane twirling like a weather vane during a pressure drop. The flags and banners of the bally-stage flutter and snap, buffeted by something that could be a change in the weather ... or could be Handsome Henry getting worked up.

"Oh, I know you well, ladies and gentlemen," he says with honeyed certainty. "You want me to tell you why it's worth your while to stick around? Why, any of these unfortunate freaks of nature deserve a dime from your pocket and a clap of your hand? I myself, an intrepid journeyer of the world's destinations of disbelief, have vowed to plant my tent-pole among you good people and never look further for life's great rewards?"

Henry flexes his long, sinewy arms, showing cannon-ball biceps. As always, his mustache is freshly waxed and his bowler is freshly brushed. As always, his body language invites his audience to the ticket booth. But to anyone who has watched the bally-man for many seasons, including Buff and Paloma, it is clear that Handsome Henry has a new spiel. Behind the tent flaps, Angelica DeMicco senses his distracted diversion. She pushes a boy with a silly face and webbed hands out onto the platform and the bally-man regards the first act of the Sideshow's Ten-in-One freakshow.

"Allow me to introduce our flipper boy, Fillip! He juggles his breakfast and scratches his nose with his toes. And for those of you who have already seen a flipper boy before, I ask you this – did you laugh or did you cry? "

Fillip does a quick back flip and retreats, waggling his ears and flapping his fins. Henry doesn't crack a smile.

"Or consider the trials of Serpentina," he says as a bronze-skinned woman steps to the stage. A massive python decorates her hips, legs and shoulders. "She is trapped in the diabolical embrace of her partner Hisssss Grace. And more than this, I promise you a Bat Boy. But he waits inside. The daylight brings out the devil in him."

Henry scans the crowd, looking for the revulsion and fear he knows lurks among the people drawn to his tent. He wants to test it. To see if he can make it run.

"Ten acts for one low price, ladies and gentlemen. That's what I am selling. Who is buying? Step right up."

There is a shuffling of feet as the men and women listening consider just how curious they are. "Then let me introduce acts five and six of our ten in one and see if they can't convince you." Bowing low, Henry ushers to the stage the pinhead and the blockhead, who caper about on the platform, knocking their misshapen noggins together until the bally-man steps between them with the order to "settle this thing inside."

"Or perhaps you would relish a look at the eight-hundred-pound lady?" he asks now. "Though I daresay, given the crop shortages and sugar spike, we'd all prefer to see the stick-girl. Nothing improves digestion like the certainty someone's hungrier than you."

A rail-thin Chinese woman steps from the tent. She brandishes a sword the size of her thigh. Henry leers. "Our sword swallower, for example, has a diet rich in iron. But you don't need to envy her either. And just wait till I introduce the fire-eater. There's some indigestion for you, holy cow!"

The audience murmurs. There is a chuckle of amusement. The bally-man's bally-hoo is working. It has pandered them, teased them, made them at ease, and now its time for Henry's final pitch.

"Ladies and gentlemen, I promised you ten amazing acts for the price of one. But today I can offer you a truly special deal. A ten-in-two. That's right. Ten phenomenal exhibits in two separate arenas. One in the light..." Henry whips off his hat with a flourish, revealing a light bulb burning under his hat. "... and one in the dark."

The line forming at the ticket booth pricks up ears.

"Magic," whispers a little boy in the crowd.

"Not magic, no," says Henry, pouncing on the reverent word. "But an opportunity you will never get again – the chance to feel in the dark what you have seen in the light. I offer you something more powerful than magic. I offer you ... human nature. "

The murmuring stops. The men shake their head, anticipating a sermon. The women furrow their brows, unable to imagine human nature among freaks of nature.

As if on cue, a sharp voice says so: "Ain't nothing natural about them!" The crowd parts to give room to the vitriol. A small woman with a pinched face, the veins on her neck popping in protest, declares: "Freaks! They're all freaks, and who needs freaks here? Send them back to wherever they came from!" The accuser searches her neighbors' faces, her eyes full of fear. She says, "Shield your eyes, God-fearing people! This is devil's work!"

In that moment, everyone in the vicinity of the Side-show feels a shift – as if the tide itself is reversing course. In that moment, Handsome Henry's dark eyes grow darker and storm clouds, darker still, press over the Rockaways with a rumble.

"Good people of Coney Island," says Handsome Henry, his voice a foghorn. "The cowering crone in your midst has spoken. These unusual specimen are not to be pitied, no. Not to be celebrated, certainly not. Not to be housed and sheltered and given work to earn their bread and butter. No. That is not in our nature. They should be sent away, she says."

He is addressing the woman who dared to point, but all of the mute men and silent women are hanging their heads, rebuked. The strange thing is, they don't even know where it comes from, this shame: Few have read the paper this morning, so they aren't thinking of the rejected refugees, turned back on the St. Louis. But they feel it, all the same – the truth of Henry's accusation: that it is easier to turn your back than to stand up tall. That they don't want the burden of the misfortunes of others. They feel the guilt of cowardice and the fear of helplessness. They feel the judgment of this carnival barker, who knows their secrets … because he knows his own.

"They can't open their arms, can't open their hearts," Henry says now, not to his audience but to the blackening sky. "They screw their eyes shut, because they don't like what they see." He lowers his gaze and addresses the offending woman: "'Send them back', you say? No. It is you who will go back. You who will run away. You who will go back to the darkness and to your own fear of the dark."

Fifty feet from the stage, away from the crowd, Paloma Bright hears the truth in Henry's voice and feels his words like a bee-sting. But Buff moves forward, more concerned for the bally-man than for the listeners he is berating.

"Henry!" he calls, but his voice doesn't carry.

Now the men and women are shuffling away from the sideshow and its sudden hostility. Some of them are already chuckling about the "crazy commie carny;" Others are steering their children hurriedly ahead of them.

"I promised you a ten-in-one," pronounces Henry to his retreating audience.

The street is empty. The bally-man shows no sign of caring. He slumps to the ground and puts his head in his hands.

Buff hurries to the side of the man who just yesterday, embodied the brash confidence of Coney Island's outrageous promises, but who now sits lost in sadness.

"Handsome?" he asks. "What the heck?"

The street is still. The man is still. An empty car creaks up the incline of the lone roller coaster on Cantilever Walk. Finally Henry speaks.

"They need to be found," he says. "The children."

He raises his head and tells Buff: "You and Paloma need to find them."

Buff is startled.

"Why us, Henry?"

"Because they vanished in broad daylight, didn't they? You are incubator babies. You know the power of light."

"The power of light?"

"Brave the dark of the day. Find the light in the night."

Buff looks over his shoulder. Paloma has not moved. Behind her, the Cyclone's train is at the crest of its peak. There are no riders, so it plunges silently.

"Has something happened, Henry?" asks Buff. "You don't seem like... like yourself."

"Because I'm not pretending," says Henry.

Buff bites his lip. Pretending, he thinks, is like wearing a mask.

"These cowards," Henry says, watching the last of the onlookers turn onto Surf Avenue in search of less judgmental entertainment. His face contorts, but his voice is not angry. "So many cowards. We're all cowards, pretending we're not scared of the dark."

A gust from the east fills the flags of the Seashore Circus Sideshow. They crack like whips, and Henry jumps.

"I'm done being a coward, Buff," he says. "I won't

run again. I meant what I said. I have planted my tent-pole and I will stand right here with you, my feet in the sand, and I won't let nothing chase me away. That's my promise to you."

Buff is not sure what to say to this. He hadn't thought that he needed such a promise.

"Believe in the light," Henry says rising to his feet. "Find the light in the night and the dark in the day. Find it. Believe in it. And they will be back. Here. Alive."

Henry picks up his cane and spins it on his palm. It balances upright and the bally-man is transformed back into the old Handsome Henry, full of cocky come-ons and pushy promises:

"They're **HERE**. They're **REAL**. They're **ALIVE**. Step inside, ladies and gentlemen – it's **SHOWTIME!**"

Buff watches Henry leap into the darkness of the Sideshow. Paloma is at his side now, and Buff can feel her suspicions.

"Maybe Handsome's got too much sun?" he says, though he knows sunlight is in short supply.

Paloma has made up her mind. "He's hiding something, Buff."

"No. He specifically said that he's not ... hiding."

Even as he says it, Buff is wondering, is that what Henry said?

"He said that it's up to you and me, Paloma. And that's, well, that's what I've been saying. Solidarity, right? Solidarity against the dark. You and me, we don't just know Coney's hiding places - we know ... he said we know about the light in the night and the ... you of all people, Paloma – the dark..."

"That stuff?" sneers Paloma. "That stuff about the light and the dark? That's just carny talk, okay? Don't let him fool you, Buff. He's a razzle artist, Henry is. Talking in riddles. It's the oldest trick in the book. Nobody better than Handsome Henry in getting you to go somewhere you only THINK you wanna go. If it's the Sideshow, ok. If it's this mysterious dark in the day, all the better. Unh unh." Paloma crosses her arms across her chest decisively. Or, perhaps, defensively. "I'm not buying it, Buff. He can bally-hoo and bally-you, but he ain't gonna bally-me."

Buff shakes his head. "You're wrong."

"I tell you. It's Handsome that's hiding something or I'll eat my hat."

"You're wrong!"

"He's probably working on some creepy kid circus act as we speak..."

"Shut up, Paloma! Shut up!"

Buff is surprised at his anger, but it's there and he lets it run through him.

"You're just sore because he said it – we're all scared of the dark. And you can't say you ain't."

He sees her flush deep, but it's Buff's lip that is trembling. He starts back up Cantilever Walk, alone.

"What are you gonna do now?" Paloma's voice says she's sorry. But she's not apologizing.

Buff bites his lip. He feels the clouds massing over the Rockaways, a black front pushing yellow into the sky like a bruise. *There are too many messages*, he thinks. *But do they all say the same thing?*

"I'm gonna look one more place." He turns and looks Paloma in the eye, daring her to tease him. "I'm going to go look where Coney's light is brightest."

And with that Buff hitches his rucksack straps tighter and heads for the Incubator Baby House.

CHAPTER SIXTEEN

In the central plaza, the overhead lights are just snapping on, spotlighting the dilapidated state of Luna Park's famous fantasy landscape: The minarets look miniature and the cupolas cowed, and Buff has the sense that Luna is sinking.

How did it happen so fast, he wonders.

Of course, 'fast' to a thirteen-year-old could be one summer or four. Anyway, it's a question that Buff already knows the answer to. At least, he knows the answer that the carnies all give: Depression. Depression, in the 1930s in America, is not something that happens to one person when times get sad. Depression is something that happens to the whole country when times get Hard.

But now it's 1939. Times should be getting better – that's what the papers say. The economy, they say, is improving. Jobs are coming out of their hidey holes. The droughts are over, the soup kitchens are not so crowded … but when Buff looks around, he still sees Depression. He sees it in the couple sitting listlessly on the Honeymoon Bench. And he sees it further up the walk, where two little girls bicker on the teacup ride as it flings their complaints in warped circles.

Buff waits warily until the girls disembark and run, still arguing, to their parents, before he continues deeper into the park.

He reaches the corner of Moonlight Walk and the rosy hue of the floodlit Incubator Baby House. Everything about the building is familiar – the crooked columns, the faded banners with their silly mustachioed cupids breaking out of a stork's egg. Buff jumps the turnstile and joins a handful of visitors gazing through the glass at the tiny babies below. They are the usual mix: a pair of young women curious at what awaits them when they would become mothers; another pair announcing, on the contrary, that no sir, you won't catch me having one of those; a few men of different ages, who simply don't associate the babies in the nursery with children at all; and there – yes, at the end of the line – is the single, aging woman who Buff knows has come to grieve. He can spot always spot them – the mothers of infants that never became children. He watches her for a moment, wondering as he always does, if she had the chance, at least, to hold her baby before it died.

On the other side of the glass, Nurse Breddy is making her evening rounds. She moves surely and efficiently among the dozen shiny incubators, adjusting the hoods and making notes on her clipboard, but a deep furrow marks her brow. She gives silent orders to two younger nurses, who nod and disappear into the linen closet. When Breddy glances up and sees Buff in the galley, she beckons. He squeezes past the visitors and down a narrow staircase to the ward below.

"Hey Breddy, Where's Doc?"

The nurse doesn't seem to hear his question. "Haven't seen such a sorry litter since we were on the road in Kansas City and that dreadful cholera took the whole lot," she says. "Not that any of them are visibly sick. They show no sign of distress, no symptoms, no rash, no labored breathing or jaundice. But it's as if they're all of them just not even a little bit willing to have at it. Like a bunch of old men lying in their beds waiting to die. I swear Buff, I can't get even one of them to open their eyes long enough to see if anyone's in there."

"What does Doc say?" asks Buff.

"Doc says the darndest things, if you don't mind my saying so. He says 'they know what's coming.' That's what he says. 'They feel a miasma,' he says."

"Did you say a miasma?" repeated Buff.

"Yep," corrected Breddy. "It's a swampy kinda condition. Not nice and easy to catch. And you know what else? Doc says maybe it means our time is up. I'm telling you Buff, he's going kinda queer. He says things I never thought I'd hear him say. Told me that maybe it was time for a change of scenery. That they had invited him to bring the babies to the World's Fair."

"The World's Fair!" exclaims Buff. "Is he going to go? Will we all go? Will you move all the babies?"

"Well I'm sure I don't know," answers Nurse Breddy. "All I know is they told Doc Couney it was time for his great contribution to medicine to be acknowledged as part of the World of Tomorrow. And Buff, I think he agrees."

"Is he here?" Buff asks.

"No. He left about an hour ago."

Buff hugs Nurse Breddy around the waist, just as he did as a toddler, and hurries back out into the gathering dark. Though not yet dinnertime, the sky is black and ominous. Buff smells a coming storm, and it smells of sulphur.

He's skirting the lagoon in the empty plaza, when he catches sight of something in the shallows. He stops and leans over the retaining wall for a better look. There, nestled among the decorative river reeds, is a small ball the color of, well, Buff couldn't say what color it is. It is not the color of the stray balls from the ball toss. It is not the color of cotton candy made grimy by small hands. It is not really a color at all, Buff decides, but it has caught his eye like a double rainbow.

Buff grabs hold of the nearest reed and shakes, dislodging the object, which splashes into the water. It sinks and joins the dark round stones on the bottom of the pool.

But when it stops sinking, Buff is amazed to see it start glowing.

There is another low rumble of thunder as Buff stretches further over the wall. In the water the mysterious object is the size of a tennis ball; out of the water it is the size of a super-sized shooter marble. In Buff's hand, it is a hard sphere of contradictions.

Wow.

He dries the orb on his shirt and turns it slowly in his palm. It is heavy and light at the same time. There are sparks on its surface and shadows in its depth. It is… compelling. But Buff can't decide if he's compelled to hide it – or throw it far away. He hears the rumble of thunder and wants only to beat the storm home. When he drops the marble into his rucksack he feels its surprising weight on his back.

Buff is almost at the park's front gate when a strange sensation overwhelms him. He feels a mist on his skin, as if he is standing close to a waterfall bathing him in spray. He turns in a circle, looking for a split hose or a sprinkler, but there is nothing out of the ordinary – just the ticket booth, the ranks of pedicabs, the garden café and there, in the corner behind the bamboo stands, the out-lines of that forgotten dark ride – the Trip to the Moon. Buff has never liked that building, a low-slung structure standing crooked to the walk with a lopsided façade. It has been hidden, unused, behind the newer attractions for a long time, and tonight it looks to Buff as though it is, itself, hiding something.

"Ring Around the Luna," he whispers. "A Trip to the Moon."

Buff feels fear rise in his throat and he swallows it. Pushing through the bamboo, he finds himself in front of the abandoned structure. He looks for the entrance into the old dark ride, but there isn't one. He circles the dilapidated building twice, searching for a window, a door, even a boarded-up hole. There is no way to get in. Buff stands still, stumped. His mind is churning out theories, supernatural conspiracies. The Trip to the Moon, he tells himself, is magic. But when he reaches out and places his palm on its thin plywood, all he gets is a splinter.

Another thunderous warning seems to shake the ground and Buff's courage fails. He crashes back through the bamboo and out the front gate, crossing Surf Avenue at a run. The sky crackles with electricity, tossing clouds across its breast in a panic. At the boardwalk, Buff stops, panting. To his left the sea swells aggressively. To his right all of Brooklyn seems to be in retreat.

He sees the moon rising pale, as if sucked into the tangled sky. It is a moon on the wane, hobbled and incomplete, and the sight of it fills Buff with profound loneliness. For a moment he feels, like the moon, to be missing a part of himself. He feels a huge sob welling inside, feels it crest like a wave breaking on the beach. He runs as fast as he can the remaining distance, pounds up the stairs into the warm lamplight of his house and yells: "Doc, I'm home."

Martin Couney looks up from his soup as both Buff and the sky over Brooklyn burst into tears.

CHAPTER SEVENTEEN

For many summers now, Doc Couney has been watching his young ward grow into a boy he loves and cares for. A boy with many endearing traits and a collection of secrets. Doc is not bothered by the secrets. They are part of Buff's independence, a self-sufficiency that makes it possible for an old man whose notion of good parenting has more to do with temperatures than temperaments, not to worry too much about the boy.

But sometimes secrets are not secrets, Doc thinks. Sometimes they are truths that must be recognized How to comfort a boy who needs more than an extra blanket and dry clothes? he sometimes wonders as he watches Buff struggle with life's injustices. How to be a good father to a boy whose life began with maternal rejection? Physical rejection. Premature ejection. Eternal...disconnection.

Last night, for example. Last night there was no reasoning with Buff, who, hours after he had stopped his unmanly bout of tears, was still hiccupping about how he must "do something." Something "in solidarity with all of them out there in the dark."

"Ach, Buff," Doc had said, patting the boy's hand. "It's a most excellent resolution and I commend it. But you must be careful – what is in solidarity in your mind, might be in solitary in action."

That's when the boy had pulled a secret from his rucksack.

"It was in the lagoon at Luna. And I think ... I think it was left for me."

When Doc Couney took the smooth, round thing in his hands, his mind wandered to the Old World – to the humid, dark, mystery of the mines. To earth, both soft and hard. And to the soil and metal and rocks of worlds unknown.

"I sink, dear boy, dis is left for no-one. I sink, on the contrary, dis is the stuff we leave. Dis is da stuff we are made of. Dis is stardust."

Now he reaches for the breadbasket and pulls the ball from the bed of dishtowels Buff had fashioned. "Remarkable," he breathes as he peers through his spectacle at the mysterious orb. The thing is larger than last night. And it has changed color - the storm in its surface has passed and it is a brighter bauble, like crystal. But it still fills Doc's hand with something both earthy and cosmic. Something like liquid heat in a satellite of ice. The scientist in him wants to take the ball into his laboratory and test it, slice it, chip it into pieces and, maybe, line his new prototype incubator with it.

But the father in him says: *Dis ball, it is Buff's.*

The clock in the hall chimes ten, but Doc decides to let the boy sleep. He places the ball back into the basket, writes a hasty note -- Beachcombing, mein Buff. Mit luck I bring back lunch -- and closes the front door behind him.

In the back lot of the Seashore Circus Sideshow, Handsome Henry rolls up his sleeves and unrolls a map. He pins both ends of the yellowed parchment with a barbell and leans forward to study the unfamiliar contours of the Coney Island coast circa 1872.

"This can't be right," he grumbles, trailing a finger along an untouched shoreline and inlets long-since filled by man and modernity. "Gotta get me a better map."

He removes one of the barbells and the map curls back across the wooden table. He replaces it with a large sheet of drafting paper and begins sketching. Twenty minutes later, his fist smudged with graphite and his coffee cold, Henry stops to survey his work. Displeased, he crumples the paper and snaps his pencil. He repeats this sequence four or five times until the roar of the Cyclone roller coaster and the clatter of the Wonder Wheel tell him it's well after opening hours. Frustrated, Henry kicks an empty paint can across the courtyard. There's a wounded bark from the fence where Yaps has been woken from his first nap of the day.

"Hm. Somebody got up on the wrong side of the bed."

Myrtle Crespi blows into the lot like a red-haired tumbleweed and winks at the bally-man. "How about you quit your football practice and take a walk down to the flea market with me, Handsome. I need a new frock for my coronation tonight."

"Can't do it, Myrtle. I'm waiting for Clyde. We've got a project. On a deadline."

Myrtle twists a long strand of hair around her finger and gets ready to whine. "Awww, Henry. Be a gentleman. I can't show up at the casino tonight in an old dress."

There's no response from Henry, who has returned to the table to sharpen his stub of a pencil with an even shorter knife. Myrtle ambles to his side and regards his work. "Taking up art lessons, Handsome? That supposed to be a boat? Or an upended Christmas tree?" She leans forward a bit. "What's with all the numbers? Code-breaking?"

Henry jerks upright and says in a voice that Myrtle doesn't recognize, "Listen, Myrtle. I don't have time for your nonsense today. No time for your smart-alec comments and sure as heck no time for your frocks."

"Well, what's got into you?" asks Myrtle. "I can see you don't have a sell-out crowd out there in front. Anyway, you're one to throw stones, ya' vain bugger..."

Henry stops her with a raised hand. It is an unusually soft hand, with polished nails. He speaks solemnly.

"There's something wicked at large, Myrtle. It's bigger than you and it's bigger than me. Now you can make yourself useful or you can take your pretty feet elsewhere. But I don't want to hear squat about no pageants nor promenades. Got it?"

Myrtle Crespi stands mortified. She has spat with plenty of men in her day – Henry included – but never has she been undone by the force of the truth the bally-man has just spoken. She shakes her head dumbly and is about to protest, "I didn't mean…" But she thinks better about starting another sentence with "I."

Instead, Myrtle lowers herself onto the bench and watches Henry stalk off into the Sideshow tent. A moment later, Angelica DeMicco emerges. She stoops to pick up Yaps and then joins the still-stunned young woman on the bench.

"He read me the riot act this morning too," she says, offering Myrtle a stick of gum. "Handsome said if I paid half as much attention to what goes on in the world as I do to my dingbat dog, we might get something accomplished."

"Accomplished?" asks Myrtle with a bite of jealousy.

Just then, Captain Clyde enters the yard, dragging several bright orange flotation devices in his wake.

"Ahoy," he calls in greeting. "Where is our Handsome leader?"

Myrtle hears Henry's voice from within the tent.

"Did you bring the winch and chain, Clyde?"

"Aye."

"The tarp?"

"Aye."

"The skiff oil?"

"Aye, Henry. I've brought it all, mate."

Myrtle turns and looks again at Henry's sketch with its mess of angles and exclamation points and what might be a lunar calendar. She recognizes among the scribbles what appears to be the Wonder Wheel and, also, the lobster cage that hangs as décor over Salty Sam's clam shack on the boardwalk. Scrawled across the top of the paper is a question: fore or aft?

Myrtle raises her head to look at Clyde with guileless eyes. "What's this then, Clyde?" she asks.

The captain of the Mickey drops his armful of marine paraphernalia and rubs his forearms.

"Well, now. Ain't we making a kid-catcher-catcher."

Again comes Henry's voice from inside the tent: "And tell that queen of the casino out there that we might be needing a mermaid!"

And Myrtle Crespi feels swell once again.

CHAPTER EIGHTEEN

It's a hot day in Flushing, Queens, and the huddle of men and one women gathered in the Trylon's long shadow are sweating through their suits. The woman shifts on her heels and waves a World's Fair commemorative fan. She quickly pockets it when one of her colleagues announces: "Here he comes now."

"More turnstiles," barks the Parks Commissioner as he marches past the cluster of aides. "I want 200,000 people passing through the Perisphere every twenty-five minutes. Double the number of trash bins on the Promenade. The World of Tomorrow must be litter-free. And for God's sake, get someone to widen the drains of the drinking fountains or we'll have unplanned swamps competing with the Lagoon of Liberty."

The Commissioner snaps a finger and the group hurries to keep up. It is his weekly inspection of his Fairgrounds and there is much to attend to. He strides past the General Automotive Palace, the Prepared Foods Dome, and the shiny blue Petroleum Building, delivering directives at every turn: "Double-check every hot-dog cart's license and revoke any that have not been personally approved ... jazz music is strictly prohibited unless commissioned by the board of composers ... get animal control agents at the perimeter to reroute migratory geese from the fairground's airspace..."

Down the Boulevard of Labor marches the Commissioner, his gaze on the Plaza of Power, where buildings that house the collective might of Capital Electric, Giant Energy and Supreme Steel hunker together like muscle-builders. Suddenly he stops. Here something he has not noticed before. It is a column, about waist-high, made of glass. It is filled with water, a single fluorescent tube, and a dozen goldfish swimming aimlessly.

"What is this?"

"That, sir, is an aqualon," answers the lady attendant brightly. "You will find them throughout the fairgrounds. They light the paths at night, and by day, they are a charming bauble. At once naturalistic and futuristic!"

The Commissioner steps up to the aqualon and taps the glass. "Bit whimsical, isn't it?"

"Pet stores are reporting increased aquarium sales this summer," notes another aide.

The Commissioner grunts. "See to it there are no fish sales anywhere on the premises. I can't abide the sight of children gripping their prize pets in cellophane bags. That's a Coney Island special, a cheap gimmick and ... tacky. I won't have it."

He returns to the paved path, but he's only taken a few steps when he looks back at the aqualon. "And I want the pebbles in those things switched out for sand," he says. "White sand. With no impurities."

By noon, the Commissioner has dispatched all of his aides to urgent tasks. He is alone at the center of the World's Fair. Alone, that is, in a sea of people. They don't recognize the Commissioner as the important man that he is, these fairgoers, and that is fine with him. He recognizes himself as an historical figure, a man whose role is too large to be seen at one glance. He watches them swim past – families and couples prattling excitedly about the Innovative Displays and Educational Presentations that he, the Commissioner, has provided. After a time, his focuses his attention on the massive statue before him. It is a gargantuan, expressionless body, and it represents Freedom. The Commissioner, a towering man himself, has to crane his neck to see the statue's blank features, but he likes it that way. Freedom, as the Commissioner sees it, is not something precious to be protected; it is something too big to topple.

"Too big to topple," he says out loud, liking its sound. He decides to use the phrase in his upcoming speech, his Independence Day speech. Such is the Commissioner's vision of freedom: imposing and authoritative, beneficial and superlative. He has been dreaming of this freedom for years. Through the hard times of the Depression and the chaos of thousands of Americans on the move, all looking for stability, a job, and their next meal, the Commissioner has been working to secure a triumphant future.

Today, he thinks, that future is here, on display.

A gust of wind stirs the branches. A flyer flutters free from a nearby information booth and fastens itself to the Commissioner's polished shoe. He leans down and removes it. He sits on a nearby bench and reads silently:

To get a glimpse into the future of this unfinished world of ours, we display for our guests the World of Tomorrow. Here, a new generation of men and women opens new fields for greater accomplishment, ensuring a brighter tomorrow. Come, let's travel to the future. What will we see? (Shows daily, on the quarter-hour, at the Perisphere.)

The Commissioner knows exactly what the visitor to the Perisphere will see: an idyllic landscape of tidy houses, clean factories, spectacular bridges, mile-high skyscrapers, dirigibles, dishwashers and highways. He has seen it himself many times from the elevated, rotating seats in the massive spherical auditorium. It is his idea of liberty: a paradise of orderly lines, automated machinery, untrammeled lawns and supervised children. But as he reads the enthusiastic words of the brochure, that perfect model world seems to recede.

The tree above him provides scant shade, but as he sits in reverie, the Commissioner feels as if a large cloud has covered the sun. A strange foreboding creeps along the walkway and sits down next to him. Forgetting his dislike for litter, the Commissioner drops the flyer on the ground. And then, he does something most unusual. He closes his eyes.

What he sees behind his closed lids is very different from the World of Tomorrow seen daily on the quarter hour in the Perisphere. He sees a world anxious and dark, full of men in uniforms and women in tears. He sees shifting borders and the smoke of bombs. War is imminent in the World of Tomorrow. But there is light too, in the Commissioner's vision. It spikes up from the surface in unlikely, unplanned spots. There is no way to control from where the light comes, and where the light goes ... it eludes even the most meticulous plans and it slips through the cracks of the heaviest steel.

With a start, the Commissioner opens his eyes in alarm. He turns and looks at the monument of Freedom. This time he sees, fluttering next to the stone man who is too big to topple, a small bird fighting against a sudden strong wind.

He stands, wipes his hands of the sweat his vision has caused, and hurries away.

Chapter Nineteen

Buff opens the door of his storytelling stall and sneezes. It's only been closed up a few days, but the booth feels as abandoned as the old Trip to the Moon building, which he has just deliberately avoided by using the back entrance of the park. Grabbing a broom from the corner, Buff gives the dusty booth a good sweep. He hangs out the **OPEN** sign, wipes down the counter looking out onto the walk, and arranges four stools on the floor. Then he opens his rucksack and pulls out the ball.

It has changed once more.

This morning, the orb had been so translucent and glassy Buff thought maybe he should take it to Madame Fortuna to ask if she had lost one of her crystal balls. But now it is milky-white like a pearl and flecked with ... what? Pepper? Sand? Buff lifts the pearl closer to his face and sneezes again. Dust?

Whatever it is, the thing is changing. It's malleable, dynamic and, Buff is inclined to think, growing. He rolls it between his palms and decides: *This is not something to share with Madame Fortuna.*

Maybe I'll show it to Paloma, if she comes by.

Maybe I'll share it with Henry.

And maybe, he thinks as he pictures Paloma's stubborn face and remembers Henry's weird warnings, I'll let it be a secret a little bit longer.

Could be better than a secret, he thinks, remembering Doc's reaction to the strange object.

Could be stardust.

Could be a good luck charm.

And so instead of wrapping it back up in its dishtowels, Buff carefully places the pearl in the empty egg carton he uses for a money-box and stashes it on the high shelf above the counter.

Sure enough, when he turns back around, one of the stools is occupied.

"Oh, hello," he says.

The girl just smiles. She's maybe six years old, with curly brown hair and a dirty dress. She puts two chubby fists on her knees and leans forward, like she wants to hear better.

"Um. Where are your folks?" asks Buff.

"They'll be back," answers the girl.

"Um. Where'd they go?" Buff leans over the counter and searches the empty walk. There are a few people at the far end, down by the Old Windmill, but they are too far to have just dropped off a child.

"They went where you go if you're gonna have to come back."

Buff scratches his head. It's a riddle, maybe. Or just a childish response. At any rate, the girl seems perfectly happy to wait for her parents. She is not alarmed and Buff doesn't want to alarm her. So he sits down on one of the stools and says, "would you like to hear a story?"

"Yes, please."

"Good. Okay." Buff clears his throat and begins the tale of the great explorer who longed to find the passage to Cathay.

"I have a friend called Cathy."

"Do you?"

"Yup. But I don't think anybody's looking for her."

"Should we be?" asks Buff warily.

But the girl doesn't answer. She just smiles and says, "Go on."

Buff glances once more at the empty walk beyond his counter. "The route to Cathay was a perilous one," he continues. "But Henry Hudson, an ambitious Englishman, knew a short-cut. Or so he thought. But there are some oceans that are not meant to be cut short, and so when Hudson and his crew found themselves becalmed on the shoals, their beautiful ship, the Half Moon, rocking just off the shore here on Coney Island ...a terrible restlessness seized the sailors and that restlessness was followed by ..."

Buff stops. It's the girl, he sees, who has been seized by restlessness. She is banging her worn leather shoes together, her eyes not on Buff, but on a spot above his head.

"You don't like the story of the Half Moon?" he asks.

"Tell me a story about that one," she says. She is pointing. Buff turns. She is pointing at his pearl. But the pearl is no longer opalescent. It is black as night, with flecks of salt, or sand, or stars.

A million thoughts beat messages in Buff's brain – too many for him to translate. He wants to grab the pearl, hide the girl, call the police, sound the alarm. He wants to shut the door, swim for the surface, sprint across sand, howl at the moon. But he ignores all these impulses and begins to tell a story. It's a story that he has never told before. One that he has never even heard before … but as it spins its way out of his mouth, he knows it is entirely his own:

"This is the story of Luna Park, the moon's nighttime playground. A playground, yes, but also the place where the moon parks her ship. This is the story about a Trip to the Moon."

The little girl has stopped fidgeting. She is listening.

"It was a trip made on a midwinter's night when no one would venture out into the cold, let alone to the moon. But on that night, a woman lay dreaming of running far, far away, and so the Luna Ship arrived to take her. And since her baby was sleeping next to her, the baby was carried on board too.

"The ship shuddered and hooted and flapped its great wings, and the mother stood at the bow with her babe in arms and together they watched their bedroom and their house and then the trees turn tiny and toy-like. The sky was dizzy with stars and when the mother looked up, she was dizzy too. She almost dropped her baby, but he clung to her, and they rose higher. The ship was following the course of a great river and the sound of the rushing water drowned out the sound of the Luna Ship's wings. The mother leaned forward to feel the spray of a great waterfall. The baby felt it too, but clung to his mother, and they rose higher.

"Soon enough the mother and her baby arrived on the moon. They say the surface of the moon is springy and the color of cheese mold. I don't know if that's true because the baby never touched it. The mother may have seen little green men with spiked heads, or the enormous laughing Moon Calf and his dancing Moon Maidens, or she may have seen something entirely different. I don't know. I do know that she shrieked with surprise and the baby shut his eyes tight. And I know that halfway through the return journey, the baby woke up and looked down on the night-dark Earth and saw a long string of lights shoot up to greet him.

"It was like a strand of Christmas against a black curtain, and as the Luna Ship descended, the lights began to dance and form secret shapes. And then the baby could see more — towers and cupolas and keen little houses atop minarets and parapets made of clouds. He saw a row of slatted mountains, running like serpents into the sea and he saw the tiny whitecaps of the surf swimming to meet them. He saw an enormous wheel turn like a giant whirligig and he twisted with it, squirming straight out of his mother's arms and over the rails of the Luna Ship.

"NOOOO...he heard her cry. But he was falling into the heart of this fairyland with its castles and lights and people and music.

"When he woke again, the baby lay in the heart of Coney Island. In Luna Park. He slept in a glass bed with a roof to keep him warm and safe. Safe from the pull of the dark space between Coney Island and the Moon."

The story is over.

Buff is holding the pearl, though he doesn't remember taking it from its shelf. His fingers burn - ashes, ashes - and his ears hum - we all fall down. He looks up from its quicksilver surface to see that the stool before him is empty. Horrified at his stupidity, he rushes out of the booth. All the way at the end of the street is the little girl. She is holding the hand of a tall woman in a stylish green suit.

"Hey!" he shouts, "who ..."

The girl turns at his voice, but the woman does not. "You can't just…" begins Buff again, but the girl just waves happily and makes a trumpet with her free hand.

"I tole ya - they'll be back!" she calls.

Now Buff sees the woman lean down and whisper into the girl's ear. Only a glimpse of the woman's profile – that's all that is visible. But he is sure that it is the face of a mother, instructing her daughter in manners.

"Thanks for the nice story," yells the little girl. Then she does a double skip and turns the corner with her mother.

Buff is alone with his lucky pearl and his made-up Luna Ship.

They'll be back, he murmurs. *Ashes, ashes…they'll all be back.*

Half Moon
June 27, 1939

*T*he Mermother floats restlessly through her den, trailing the threads of a net she has begun to weave. It is a net she hopes she will not have to use, because the floor of the carousel is already covered. Now there are five children sleeping on the sand. She lingers over each one, adjusting the bubbles that pillow their heads.

It's been a week since she plucked her crown jewel for delivery, a week since the boy discovered her pearl. The Mermother had known to expect that things on land could get worse before they got better, but she was dismayed when another child had to be rescued. She is a sweet little girl with curls, whose parents spend all their time waving placards down at the dock, shouting, "No room for refugees, no jobs for Jews."

One day, the little girl got tired of waiting for them to come home, and the Mermother had to act.

Passing into the shell of the old observatory, the Mermother arrives at the small opening that telescopes the sky into her den. She sees the moon – a clean wedge, sliced in half. To the east, the bright lights of the Sideshow are burning long into the night. The Mermother recognizes the bright flame of a vigilante, but she is not sure of its source. She knows that fuel - like the bally-man's guilt - can burn just as quick as it heats. Has the bally-man struck a spark? Or lit a match?

And then there is the shadow over the Bowery, where a friendship smolders against suspicion. And there is anxiety at the police precinct, where frustration and fear feed themselves.

Rising closer to the surface, the Mermother searches the sky for the ring that marks the moon's dark side, but another source of light is blocking it out. It is the electrified Funny Face, the same grinning specter that she has been watching all week with growing uneasiness. In the mornings, the Funny Face goes cross-eyed. The left eye rolls in its socket to follow a small boat trudge slowly around the Point and north up the Narrows towards Flushing, leaving behind the smell of sabotage. But at night, it has both eyes open – vigilant with malice. Its wide mouthed grin is poised for an insult. The Mermother hisses a single shush through the waves, and its heavy lids slam shut.

Settling back onto the seafloor, the Mermother gathers a handful of sand. She watches it spill, grain by grain, through her long blue fingers. The boy is young, she thinks, and that's why I chose him. But time is running out.

She beats her heavy tail in syncopated impatience. She holds one hand to her mouth and utters a single note – faaaa – that ripples through the water.

In a moment a sleek creature is at her side.

Fetch the boy, she says. And the blue-black dolphin slips soundlessly away.

CHAPTER TWENTY

It is nearly daybreak and Buff is awake. He doesn't sleep so well anymore. Not since he smelled the Miasma in the Steeplechase warehouse. Not since he argued with Paloma. Not since Henry told him to find the lost children but, instead, he went and let another one get lost. It didn't matter that somehow Buff knew that she was safe, the little girl who had skipped happily away from his story-telling booth holding the green lady's hand; She had been reported missing the very next day and Ramsey was at his wits end.

So much for good-luck, he thinks as he reaches a hand under his pillow and wraps his fingers around the cold orb, which is now the size of a croquet ball.

I shoulda chucked it in the creek.

Buff listens to the steady breath of the surf outside his window and turns his attentions to the sounds inside. He cues the creaking floorboards and the ticks and tocks of a dozen clocks. Soon, the whole house falls into the easy rhythm of his beating heart. A familiar melody fills his ears:

Ring around the Luna…
Pocket full of tuna…
Ashes, ashes…
We all…

The song is interrupted by the bang of the window shutter springing open. A bright shaft of light is fingering its way over the sill and across the bed's thin quilt. Buff feels it on his legs, a cool stream in the humid night. He watches the ribbon of light drip over the side of the bed and stretch along the floor towards the stairs. Now he is more than awake; Buff has jumped out of bed.

Quietly, he follows the slippery beam past Doc's closed door and down the stairs and out onto the porch. He takes a deep breath. The air is clear, free of the soggy stench that has plagued his days and his dreams. The beam expands and grows brighter – it's a pathway to the beach and beyond. Buff runs down its ribbon like a sea turtle making for safety.

When he's nearly at the waterline he sees it: out in the center of the weird spotlight, an enormous dolphin leaps into the air with a greeting — *faaaa.*

Buff feels this cry like adrenaline. Filled with some-

thing he wants to believe is courage, he calls back. The dolphin leaps again and surges through the water, racing parallel to the beach. Without a thought, Buff follows on land. The sand is cool on his feet as he runs all the way to Steeplechase Park. At the Pavilion of Fun he glances up at the Funny Face, ready to challenge the bullying smile, and sees its eyes closed under heavy steel lids. With a shout of delight, Buff lifts a fist and keeps running. Breathless and exhilarated, he arrives at the Dreamland Pier. At its far end, the dolphin executes a final pirouette above the water and then disappears. So does the mysterious light. But Buff knows where they have gone.

He clambers onto the rickety remains of the pier and navigates the slippery pylons over the water. When he reaches the last of the decapitated columns, his pajamas are wet to the knees. Wondering why he has never ventured here before, he waits, his eyes on the buoy-bell bobbing a hundred yards in front of him. Buff sees the water around the buoy bubble and churn ... and a luminous creature emerges from the deep. It is a woman beautiful and bold, her hair a mass of phosphorescence crowned in a simple ring of pearls. Her skin is alabaster, with veins

of blue, and her eyes are warm green gems.

As she hovers at the surface, Buff sees her green-gold tail and understands that he is in the presence of a mermaid.

He bows his head. She speaks and her voice rings out like bells.

I am the Mermother. I offer the moon as solace and protection. My powers wax and wane. They are always at work with the sea and the tides. But Coney Island, like all earthly creatures, needs the strength of sunshine.

Buff raises his eyes. He wants to answer, but he can't find his voice.

You are my emissary of the sun, my messenger of warmth. You must help me restore these to land, so Coney Island can survive these times of spiritual scarcity.

The Mermother lifts her arms from the water, scattering droplets like diamonds. Brass rings run from her elbow to her shoulder and a thick rope of emerald algae decorates her pale blue throat. On her head is a crown. Buff sees a hole in its ornate tiara – a hole where his pearl once was.

"It's your pearl," he says, marveling. "I have your..."

You have all that you need, the Mermother confirms. *I chose you, because your heart shines bright. And because you feel your home's pulse in your blood. That is why I left it for you to deliver.*

"I will take care of it, I promise," says Buff eagerly. "I won't let anything happen to it."

But the Mermother shakes her head. *It is much more than a beautiful bauble, and you are much more than its guardian. You must do more than keep it safe. You must nourish it. You must fill it. Fill it with the future. That's what it is – that mysterious, changeable thing. It is Coney's future, and you must prove that it is … viable.*

The Mermother lifts her face skyward.

When there is no moon to light the way – that is when your heart must shine. She returns her warm green gaze to Buff's. *Have hope. Have courage. Believe in the light in the night. Believe in the promise of tomorrow.*

With that, the creature vanishes. As she does, the sun peeps above the Rockaways and the half-moon bows lower. Buff stands on the last stump of the ruined Dreamland Pier, stunned. He is alone and half-naked, and he holds in his clenched fist the Mermother's pearl.

When Paloma opens her front door to let out the cat, she laughs out loud. There stands Buff, clad only in pajamas and a bewildered smile. He is clutching what might be a greasy knish bag. It's not the first time her friend has appeared unexpected and barefoot on her steps, but this morning when she lets him in, she ushers a truce in as well.

Buff takes a seat in the kitchen and wordlessly accepts dry socks and a cup of tea. Paloma glances at the bag, waiting for him to offer her breakfast, but Buff is lost in thought. She fills the sink to wash up last night's dishes and starts talking to fill the silence.

"You shoulda heard the debate out my window last night, Buff. Two soused sods arguing over what's the best model of gramophone. One of em says to the other, 'you couldn't get sausage out of that horn, let alone Benny Goodman' so the other one starts defending his Victrola by beating the other guy senseless, singing some squawking aria the whole time. Geez, it was funny. I nearly had to add my two cents – thought maybe if I threw my harmonica collection out the window at them it would settle the argument, but…"

"Do you think there's magic on Coney, Paloma?"

Paloma turns off the water and considers the question.

"Magic? What kinda magic? I mean, you and me both know how Sir Crustacle does his conjuring act. That's not magic. That's Coney razzle dazzle. Sleight of hand. Smoke and mirrors. That what you mean?"

"No," says Buff, shaking his head slowly. "That's not what I mean."

He pushes his half-empty mug aside and rustles the paper bag. Paloma dries her hands and pulls a chair close. Buff opens the bag and shows her what lies inside. It is not a knish at all. It is small and opalescent. It shimmers. It glows.

Paloma studies it without touching.

"That's one spooky egg," she concludes.

An egg.

Of course.

Not a bauble.

"Where did you find it?"

Buff considers the possible answers.

In the lagoon.

In my fist.

In a mermaid's crown.

"I got woken up this morning by a dolphin," he finally says.

"A dolphin," repeats Paloma.

"Yeah. I think maybe it brought it."

Paloma prods the egg. It wobbles under her touch.

"Dolphins lay eggs?" she asks.

Buff steadies the pearl, squeezes it lightly with his thumb. It gives off an electric shock.

Prove it's viable.

Coney's future.

"So, if it's an egg…" he begins.

"It will hatch."

"Yes. It will hatch."

They sit in silence, their thoughts swirling on different planes until they collide and Paloma and Buff say at the same time: "Doc."

CHAPTER TWENTY-ONE

Buff bursts into Doc's cluttered office in the Incubator House with Paloma on his heels. The old man looks up from his books and says, "So. Tell me mein child: To where did you slip from your bed in such wee hours und why are you looking so shell-shocked on return? And did you by chance see the de remarkable sunrise dis morning dat was, meteorologically speaking, most unlikely?"

Buff clears a space on Doc's desk and deposits the egg. To his surprise, it is about twice the size it was when they left Paloma's place. He glances at Paloma and takes a deep breath before saying. "It's an egg. But not a dolphin's ... egg."

Then, as Doc examines the sparking sphere and Paloma gawps in amazement, Buff spills a strange narrative of undersea hatcheries, elusive mothers, magic, hope and the future.

"Oy," Doc responds when he is finished.

"That kind of magic," whispers Paloma, sitting down heavily on a couch covered in papers and oxygen canisters.

"I know it sounds crazy," stammers Buff. "But doesn't everything that happens down here on Coney?"

"Umm. Not that crazy," says Paloma.

"What do I do, Doc?" asks Buff.

"You hatch de egg, dat is most clear. We incubate de egg, because dat is vat we know how to do."

"But is incubating a..." Buff pauses, embarrassed. "Is incubating a mermaid's egg as easy as incubating a newborn baby?"

"Oh. I very much sink no. No it is not."

From the sofa comes the sound of Paloma smacking her forehead in disbelief.

"For one ting," continues Doc, unperturbed. "Dis ting, whatever it is going to be – maybe turtle, maybe turtle dove, maybe animal or maybe mineral or vegetable or heck, maybe cheese - whatever it is, it is not ... yet. Mit ein kinder, well, it already is what it will be. The baby-varmers can only make sure it stays zat way. But dis ting? Maybe what it is going to be depends on conditions. Depends on its incubation."

"Its future," clarifies Buff.

"Perhaps. Yes. Perhaps it depends on what you want it to be."

Paloma blows her bangs from her face. It sounds like exasperation. "C'mon Doc," she protests. "You saying this is some kind of hocus-pocus egg? Say the magic words and you get a white rabbit?"

"I'm saying dat one man's science is another man's magic. Look at you two. You are de opus of science – de science dat makes a seed grow and bear fruit. Science dat few recognize as ze magic it is, unless they take time to watch it unfold. Take, for anozzer example, de slogan of de World's Fair. An empty boast, is it not? 'Mankind is New and Improved in de World of Tomorrow.' Because we know dere is nussink new in men, and women, striving for improvement. Science is not de new magic, my friends. It is de oldest of magics. Moreover – magic itself will always be a science, ever studied, ever mastered, ever mystifying."

Buff is quiet as he tries to reconcile this philosophy with the possibility that he is in possession of a mermaid's egg in need of a warm bed. Paloma creeps forward to peek over Buff's shoulder at the thing.

"What I saw this morning. It was magic," Buff says. "It was Coney Island magic."

"What you saw this morning," argues Paloma, "has a scientific name – delirium. Right, Doc?"

"Coney Island," says Doc, as he pulls a magnifying glass from his desk to better examine the egg, "is like a marvelous factory, where nobody knows what is ze product. Here, de workers, dey make wonder — Wonder Wheels. And de steel dey use suspends not bridges — but disbelief."

Doc puts down the glass and picks up the orb. He moves to the window and holds it to the light.

"Let me tell you about the de man dat built Luna Park. When I came to him mit my idea for dis child hatchery, I spent much hot breath to tell about anatomical development and skeleton structure and body temperature, et cetera, et cetera." Doc turns the pearl in his hand, studying its translucence. "Do you know vat he told me? He told me: 'easy mit de science, Doc. Science sounds pricey and it don't sound fun.' He meant dis: people come to Coney Island for the de thrilling-ness. So, he said, use science to scare dem from out of their pants. And I saw what he meant when he built de Luna Ship. You know de one? That ride – the Trip to the Moon – it had the lines dat never ended."

Buff sits up straighter at the mention of the dark ride.

"I was just thinking about that!" he exclaims. "About the Trip to the Moon ride. Just the other day, I was wondering – what kind of a ride it was, you know, back then?"

"Oh it was most popular!" answers Doc. "Day after day und night after night, crowds came and vaited for a chance to embark on a toy ship to de moon. Of course dey knew dat little green men would come at the end and take dem to an exit door dat opened up onto shooting gallery and de photo stand. But inside of de dark, grown men and grown women clutched each udder in delight. And de delight came from confused tinking -- zey were going to see...the unknown. An unknown that was both scientifically and technically possible ... but also impossible."

Buff looks serious. A week ago, The Trip to the Moon might as well have made a one-way journey for all he knew or cared. But now it's pushed its way into made-up stories and history lessons.

"But it's just a building," he says, his voice unsure. "Not a proper ride. I mean there was no actual Luna Ship, and you couldn't actually travel above the earth ... or fall out of it ..." Buff sees Paloma looking at him funny and he trails off, confused.

But Doc just chuckles and holds a finger aloft. "Dat was de magic. A little somesink called imagination."

"Nobody goes on that worn-out ride anymore," says

Paloma with a dismissive wave. "People want to see the World of Tomorrow nowadays, not some ragged old imaginary moonscape."

Doc Couney is holding the pearl to his ear as if it's a seashell with a message from the ocean. "Ja, ja," he nods. "The World of Tomorrow is somesink at which we dare not sniff."

He shifts the egg from his ear to his nose and inhales. "But I sink, too, we must not sniff at Buff's sea-friend. For she is a manifestation not of magic, and not of science, but of somesink in between. Somesink dat knows dere is no rosy-dawning tomorrow wizzout zere is a deep, dark night."

With that, the old scientist blows on the egg and polishes it on his sleeve as if it were his spectacles. It turns a new shade of blue, a celestial blue.

"Luna," he says and chuckles. "A little moon."

There is a knock and Nurse Breddy's perspiring face appears at the door.

"Ah. Just in time you are, Breddy," says Doc as he places the egg back on the desk. "Vould you be so kind as to help Buff with this ... curiosity? Ve are keen to find out if maybe zere is a little man in zis little moon."

CHAPTER TWENTY-TWO

To the north of the gargantuan Freedom monument, past the Railroad Building and down a sloping lawn from the People's Expressway is an area of the fairgrounds that the Commissioner has expressly avoided on his inspection tour. It is the Midway, a selection of rides and games that the Commissioner had allowed to be installed at the Fair as a concession to "popular will" – that distasteful and misguided force that he knew, as a city official, must be reckoned with delicately.

It is as Paloma Bright has declared: the amusements of the World of Tomorrow offer a very muted sort of thrill in comparison to those of old Coney Island. There is, as she has supposed, a small pond on which rowboats can be rented and a few mild-mannered mechanical rides presenting a modicum of enjoyment for the very young. None of these attractions advertises itself with much enthusiasm. Their existence is noted perfunctorily on the visitors' maps with a note that they operate on a "limited schedule." Even their physical presence, located far below the sightline of the main entrances, indicates their secondary status in the spectrum of the Fair's attractions.

With one exception.

The Parachute Jump, the tower that Officer Ramsey has heard tell about, has just been erected, and its distinctive top – a broad canopy of steel rods holding a ring of parachutes ready to descend, is more than visible. It is a real attraction. A curious crowd gathers at the small entry to the Midway to watch the tower being turned into an unprecedented and novel thrill ride.

Among them is Mingus Lamont, who smells an opportunity.

Wiggling his way through the Fairgoers and past a few security guards, Lamont arrives at the bottom of the Parachute Jump already talking.

"Just the thing. Double-reinforced grappling hooks that will cut the time for loading and unloading in half," he explains to the foreman in charge of the new ride. "See, what you have here," he continues, fingering one of the seats awaiting attachment to the tower's pulley, "is a three-step contraption that will slow you down every time you need to let one off and put a new one on."

"Well, sure," answers the foreman. "You need the lap belt to keep them on the bench, a winch to hold it level, and a harness to keep the bench steady with the chute."

He squints at the Coney Island carny. Plenty of experts have inspected the Jump, an altogether new sort of ride that lifts passengers hundreds of feet into the air and then drops them in a gentle and guided fall to earth under an expanded chute. They have all marveled at the Jump's complex system of cables and supports and nodded in approval of its safety. Lamont is the first observer to suggest a time-saving adjustment. He's not averse to it, the foreman, since he knows that when the Jump is operational in a few days' time, he and his crew will be confronted with a long line. He has already worried that they will not be able to keep up.

Lamont senses an opening and pulls from his pocket the mechanism in question. The foreman inspects it and then, experimentally, switches the network of clasps on one of the benches for the grappling hook. Mingus Lamont quickly climbs onto the bench and demonstrates the ease with which he can release and secure himself to the parachuted lift. "Not bad, eh?" he winks.

The foreman hesitates. He looks up at the tower and considers worst case scenarios. "I dunno," he says. "There's a lot riding on these benches."

"Tell ya what," says Lamont, scrambling from the seat. "There's a case of these hooks down at the marina. I brought 'em up myself this morning. Send one of your men down to pick it up. Try it out. If you're not one hundred percent satisfied, you owe me nothing. And if you use 'em when it comes time to keep the line moving, well

... just tell the Commissioner that Steeplechase came through for you again. The hooks are, as they say in the finest establishments, gratis."

The foreman is looking up again at the top of the Parachute Jump. He watches as, one by one, the sky-high benches drop, the unfurling chutes that slow them drifting like clouds in a hot blue sky. He rubs his chin and turns to shake hands with the unsolicited offer, but Mingus Lamont is already gone. He is headed back to the lonely marina on Flushing Bay where he has docked the Miasma.

At this same moment, Handsome Henry returns from his lunch to the back lot of the Sideshow. His stomach full and his mind refreshed, the bally-man considers the contraption sitting in the middle lot. He's had a number of false starts, but he has finally, he thinks, hit upon the right design. A simple trap. To catch a kid-catcher.

There are just a few more details to work out, and the decision about where to lay his trap. On the boardwalk? On the pier where the Miasma docks? Somewhere low down and dirty where only that rotten Mingus Lamont haunts? And then of course, the question of what to use for bait. Or rather, who to use for bait. His mind flashes to Buff and Paloma, the only kids he trusts.

No, thinks Henry. *That's not the answer.*

Not, he tells himself, because he's worried about putting them in danger. They are not the right kind of bait. Buff and Paloma, he thinks, are elemental Coney Island. They cannot be stolen anymore than all of the sand on the beach can be stolen. Any more than all the memories of summer can be stolen. Any more than ... Henry sits down heavily, his enthusiasm dimmed. He looks up at the pale grey sky and the haze of its heavy expanse. Any more than the sun can be stolen, was what he was thinking.

Henry lays a hand over his eyes. The idea that Buff and Paloma could be in danger surfaces like a horrible ghoul in a dark ride. Right behind it is an even more frightening specter – the possibility that he might fail them in their hour of need. It's a thought that has haunted him, he realizes, for days. Since the day the St. Louis was turned away and ignored. Since the day Buff came dancing the blues. The St. Louis blues.

Hate to see the sun go down. 'Cause my baby done left town...

The bally-man jumps up with a shout that he is glad there is no one to hear. He turns to his half-built contraption in desperation. Only the completion of his kid-catcher-catcher can ease his conscience and his guilt. He rushes to the pile of hardware and blueprints with the single-minded resolve of a man obsessed.

"Gah!" he shouts, and in that one oath is hope almost lost. Because the crate of grappling hooks that he had lugged to the yard that morning to finish the trap ... is gone.

CHAPTER TWENTY-THREE

Rita Chervinsky has only just arrived at her fortune-telling parlor and already she's considering going back to bed. When she got up this morning, still unrested, Rita forecast a hot, heavy day. She takes no satisfaction in her accurate prediction. Now she stands on the mezzanine of the nearly empty theater, sweating and surly, and resolves to put her crystal ball away forever. Just as soon as she finishes this last gig.

"Enough is enough," she mutters with a glance at the lacquered box on the shelf. Her palms itch with the need to count again the stack of bills inside. The stack that doubled in thickness after Mingus Lamont's unexpected visit last week. With that kind of money, thinks Rita, I can retire to the country. Find a little cottage, upstate. Somewhere quiet. With cows, maybe.

She starts for the box but the sound of footsteps on the floor below stops her. Leaning over the railing, she sees Handsome Henry, the Sideshow barker, standing in the empty lobby.

"Can I come up?" he asks.

Rita studies the face looking up at her. Her own children are grown now, older even than the bally-man. But something in his face feels like the tug of young hands on her apron. She waves for him to follow and enters her parlor.

When they are sitting across from each other at the small round table, Madame Fortuna says, "Well? I don't suppose you're here to find out if there's a rich man in your future."

Henry scoots forward in his chair. "Did anybody come to you?" he asks. "Ask for your help? Help finding the lost kids?"

"Sure," shrugs the fortune-teller. "Officer Ramsey came by every time one of 'em went missing. I looked in the ball, I did. But I didn't see nothing but bubbles."

"Bubbles, huh?"

"Bubbles. Sometimes it does that." She shrugs again. "It's got a lotta years on it, that ball. It's near as old as me. Cracks in the crystal, constant indigestion, agida—what have you. But it don't matter. Customers think the bubbles look mysterious."

"Yeah, but I don't mean Ramsey," says Henry with a shake of his head. "What I mean is the mothers. Did they come to you? Did they ask? Did they think you could see where they mighta went?"

Then, before she can answer, Henry leans all the way

across the table. "Tell my fortune, Rita?" he whispers.

She cocks her head slightly, unsure what to think of this. Handsome Henry, she knows, doesn't believe in Madame Fortuna's clairvoyance any more than she believes his claims to have "sailed the seven seas to bring Coney Island the spectacles of the Sideshow."

"What is it?" she asks, suspicious.

"Maybe we can find them."

"The missing kids?"

"The mothers," he whispers, dropping his chin to his chest.

The fortune-teller studies the bally-man. He seems wounded, she thinks. Like his whole soul is limping. She pushes the crystal ball from the center of the table and reaches for Henry's hand. He opens it wide for her to see. She holds his wrist between her thumb and index finger and feels his racing pulse. Then she rubs her thumb upwards, watching his fingers part. Here is a fork in the road, she understands. And there is a right way and a wrong way.

Madame Fortuna drops Henry's hand and rises from the table. She stands before the box with its stack of bills. Two hundred dollars. It's enough, she knows. Enough to let her go home to bed. Enough to board a train north. But then what, Rita?

She turns back to the bally-man. She sees now what he hasn't shown anyone. She knows she can't see the future anymore than Henry can, but she is a mother and she can see a son's pain. Even when it is long in the past. She picks up Henry's hand once more and notes the calluses and ink-stains.

"You are trying to right a wrong, I see. A lapse in judgment. An omission of kindness."

Henry's eyes dart wildly, searching his own hands for the truth that Madame Fortuna reads there.

"I see you building a scaffold," she continues. His head jerks up.

"You can see that?"

Rita nods. She doesn't mention that she has been watching the Sideshow lot from the mezzanine window for days. She doesn't say that it was Mingus Lamont who stole the grappling hooks from the yard and that the moment she saw him do it, she knew that she must not take the money. The Steeplechase manager has chosen the wrong path, and she knows she cannot follow him. She knows she will not be buying a cottage upstate anytime soon. As for the handsome bally-man, she is not sure how to help him.

"It's a desperate plan," she says. "The one you are working on."

"But will it work?"

"Depends on what you want it to do."

"Keep the kid-catcher from running," says Henry.

Rita nods to herself. She has read his palms, but the truth is in his eyes. She knows that it is himself that Handsome Henry is trying to keep from running.

CHAPTER TWENTY-FOUR

When Nurse Breddy arrives at the Incubator Baby House the next morning, she is greeted with the sound of gurgling infant contentment. Three junior nurses are rushing about busily, changing blankets and bottles.

"I'd say they've turned a corner, ma'am," says one when she sees Breddy's astonished face. "They've had us running ragged the past hour, the hungry things. I've never seen anything like it. Except maybe that time Paloma Bright set a half-pound bag of catnip in the alley and the strays went bonkers. I dunno what got into them, but they're sure a happy bunch now."

Nurse Breddy inspects the bassinets in mounting disbelief. Every single one of the newborns is bright-eyed and awake, complexions rosy and toes all a-wiggle.

She makes her way down the aisle, tucking and clucking, until she comes to the curtain behind which she and Buff have installed his unusual arrival. She pauses for a moment and then pulls the curtain aside.

Buff is sitting beside the bassinet, looking weary.

"It didn't hatch," he says.

"No," says Breddy. "But it appears to be having an excellent influence on the babies." She waves down the row of kicking cherub feet. Buff leans back for a better view.

"Oh," he says with a grin. "How about that?"

"How long have you been here, young man?"

"I slept here. Sort of. I was … keeping it company. I mighta fallen asleep."

Now Buff taps the glass enclosure that holds the fate of Coney Island and repeats to himself the mysterious instructions: *Nourish it … fill it with hope.*

He was trying.

Doc's lecture about the magic of science (or was it the science of magic?) had convinced Buff that he – a kid with little more to offer than a slew of good stories – could indeed be a midwife to some sort of miracle. And so he spent the whole night nurturing the egg, filling it with the sound of his voice. Starting with the legend of Henry Hudson's ill-fated crossing, Buff made his way through his entire repertoire of Coney Island lore. In the quiet corner of the Incubator House he told stories of brigands and ballerinas and a three-legged stork. He watched sticky filaments swim through the pearl as he told it about the jellyfish that breached the Venetian Lagoon; he saw flutters of white feathers appear as he described the arrival of carrier pigeons in the middle of Luna Park with messages from all over the world. There was the tale of the old woman who held up an armored car with knitting needles and the drifter who taught the Pygmies of the Jungle to speak French. By the time he had finished the story of the organ grinder who, on his death, left a small fortune to his monkey, the Mermother's pearl had once again doubled in size and was as warm as a winter potato.

At dawn, Buff had only one story left. He told the story of the Luna Ship and the Trip to the Moon, and then he slept.

Now he rubs his eyes and frowns at the quiet gray-green pearl.

"Well, these things take time, you know," says Breddy. "Why don't you go have some breakfast with Doc? I brought in a batch of muffins. He's in his office eating all them all up. I'll watch over this ..." She doesn't know what to call it. She moves towards the bassinet but stops. She doesn't know the first thing about burping an egg

Doc Couney is at his desk, hidden behind a pile of books on which rests a plate of half-eaten muffins. Buff chooses the least nibbled and flops down on the sofa by the door. He eats silently and then brushes the crumbs from his lap with a sigh.

"Come now, Buff. Out wid dese deep thoughts, if you please," says Doc from behind his books. "I can't hear myself tink for all your ... internal debate."

Buff just sighs again. "Breddy says the babies are much better this morning. Do you think that means something?"

"Indeed I do. I tink it means dey got a good night's sleep." Doc looks up over his books at the boy sitting forlornly across the room and puts his teasing aside. "So," he says with a clap of his hands. "The moon-egg?"

"Overcast," answers Buff. "Though it's bigger. And, different. I can't say how exactly. But different. I spent all night talking, but I was also listening. Like a safecracker at a stubborn lock. But I couldn't crack it. Every time I thought I was close …"

"It grows warm and den cold and den quiet and den buzzy," nods Doc. "But it has not hatched. So. How to make action out of waiting, ja Buff? This is the trick."

Buff is quiet. He doesn't want to point out that yesterday Doc had said the real trick was "a little thing called imagination." Because that's what Buff is afraid of after another unusual night. That this can all be explained as an overactive imagination getting the better of him. Not just the change in the pearl…but the pearl itself and its mysterious origin. He's afraid that Doc is just humoring him. That Paloma, with her shouts of "Delirium! Hallucinations! Crazy-town!" is right.

But Doc is already at his bookcase, pulling out more tomes to add to the precarious stacks around his desk.

"Biology of the Egg… Ovi-oxidation und de Fetus,"

he reads as he scans the shelf. "Fortpflanzung die Menschlich... Thermal Regulation of Reptile Incubation. We have many resources at our hands, Buff."

Buff pulls his feet up onto the couch and closes his eyes. Doc's voice ("Die Zygote und Sie ...Iatrogenic Transmission in Utero ...Miracles of the Midway: a Discourse on Audience Enthusiasm.") is lulling him back towards sleep, until it is interrupted by a knock at the door.

"Ja wohl," answers Doc, his head bent over one of his favorite texts, Raptors of Croatia.

"You have a visitor," says Nurse Breddy. She stands aside and a woman whose smart suit and leather briefcase indicate business steps into the room.

"Doctor Martin Couney?" asks the visitor.

"Indeed, I am," agrees Doc. "Please have a seat." He gestures to a small chair, the only one in the room free of books and papers. "Muffin?" he offers. The woman sits, shakes her head at the crumby plate, and pulls a sheet of paper from her briefcase.

"Doctor Couney, it is my great pleasure, as a standing member of the Committee for Participant and Exhibitor of Inclusivity, to present you..."

"But you are sitting," Doc interrupts.

"Sir?"

"You are, at least at present, a sitting member of dis committee." The old man chuckles at his joke.

The woman's face softens. "Yes. Well. It is my pleasure to present you with an invitation to move your Incubator Babies to the World's Fair for the summer season."

Behind her, Buff sits up straight and throws a wild eye at Doc. But Doc is not looking at him. He is looking at this woman and her official paper with its formal invitation.

"You won't be disappointed, Doctor Couney," she continues. "It is high time your accomplishments were recognized. Heavens – such progressive methods should be on display at New York's finest hospitals! Not among the quackery that Coney Island is famous for. All you need to do is sign here," she points to the paper, "and here. And we will expedite the process of installation."

Doc's face undergoes an exaggerated display of thoughtfulness. He says, "It is most velcome –your support, Madam. But it is, should I say, premature, dis paper you bring. Not of course, dat I am frightened of tings dat come prematurely! On contrary, it is, my specialty." He chuckles. "Only but I do take concern about de labor and upheaval of moving my little baby factory, you see. Because dey are much more perishable dan, say, wireless radios and refrigerators and electric cars and whatever else you are exhibiting at the World of Tomorrow."

"Oh, but we will provide you with whatever careful preparations and transport you require," asserts the woman briskly.

"Again. Most kind of you. Dis support," nods Doc. "But you see, I have always been very careful not to permit dese little achievements of mine become …how shall we say, exploited for purpose of a triumph dat dey do not yet need to be part of, you agree?"

The woman frowns. It is not clear if she agrees. Or even if she understands what she is being asked to agree with.

"Well Doctor Couney, if you would prefer to arrange things without advertising and promotional opportunities, we can certainly accommodate that. But please keep in mind that the Fair has already run through half its season. There are only a few months left. We are fortunate that we can even offer you this opportunity. You see, some valuable real estate has been made available – due to the Government of Germany's decision not to participate."

Doc Couney's polite resistance is gone.

"*Mein Gott*," he explodes. "Surely you do not mean to say dat you are now accommodating de 'decisions' of Germany. For dat is not a Government to be accommodated. Dat is nussink but a tyrant. I don't know vat you do in City Hall or in Queens, but here in Brooklyn we do not acknowledge dat man's decisions."

The woman shifts uneasily in her chair. "Of course. I meant to say that it was the Commissioner's decision. To persuade the German Chancellor." She shifts again, choosing her words carefully. "To persuade the Chancellor to forego the privilege of participation. The privilege we would now like to extend to you," she finishes rather lamely.

Buff's head is swimming. He knows that they are speaking of Hitler, the German dictator. The one with the shrill, shrieking voice and herky-jerk swagger. The one from the newsreels. The one who has forced people from their homes and onto boats, looking for refuge. He thinks of the tiny babies in their incubators. He imagines rocking with the sway of the sea.

"Chancellors, Commissioners – dey are such deceitful names, are dey not?" Doc mutters now. "I do not care for ultimatums, madam, nor for privileges."

He takes his spectacles from his nose and rubs them on his sleeve. When he replaces them, he studies the woman sitting before him. She is a well-meaning woman, he thinks. Guileless, but careless.

"I do see much to admire in your Fair, madam. However, I have not actually seen your fairgrounds and so, technically speaking cannot admire what I have seen. Not. You see." Doc coughs at the complexity of his explanation and Buff gets to his feet. He feels the small pit in his stomach that has been telling him that his egg is a dud and that mermaids are fantasies. He hears the voice in his head whispering:

Ultimatum.

Oviraptor.

Victory, quackery.

But above these doubts and clear as a bell comes the liquid voice of the Mermother:

Fill it with the future. The promise of tomorrow.

Buff clears his throat, startling the woman with his sudden presence. "I believe that what Doctor Couney is suggesting," he says, "is that he would be more inclined to entertain your invitation if he could visit the Fair in advance ... with his expert advisors."

The woman hesitates only a moment and then withdraws another envelope from her briefcase, which she hands to Buff.

"But of course. Here is a pass to the Fair. Please come and see for yourself."

She turns again to Doc, who is watching this exchange with interest.

"We will gladly arrange for a tour for you and your party, Doctor. Or you may visit the Fair alone. But we do need your answer by the end of the week."

When their visitor is gone, Doc Couney smiles at his self-appointed expert advisor. "It seems," he says, "we have a date mit de Vorld of Tomorrow."

Crescent Moon
July 1, 1939

*T*he children gallop wildly on imaginary horses. They are in high spirits, and the Mermother knows why. They are forgetting the troubles they left on land. They are forgetting, she knows, everything they left on land.

This is not what she intended.

"Gather round," she tells the children as they tumble from their make-believe ride. "Gather round, we are going to play a new game."

She smoothes a wide patch of sand before them and hands each child a sea urchin quill.

"Let's draw a picture of Coney Island," she says.

In an instant the children are bent over their work and familiar shapes emerge: the Wonder Wheel, a roller coaster, a forest of beach umbrellas and a train of lemonade carts. Relieved, she offers another suggestion: "Let's put your families in the picture, shall we? Because wouldn't they enjoy it too?"

Again the children set to their sandy canvas, adding bits that any artist would think creative and inspired, but fill the Mermother with fresh concern. Because the Coney Island of her rescued children is now populated with seahorses carrying picnic baskets and jellyfish pushing baby carriages.

"Mary Lou," she says gently. "Could you draw your mother's face a bit larger? So I can see her smile?"

But Mary Lou looks at her in confusion.

"My mama doesn't smile," she says. Then she turns back to the sand picture and inserts among the sea creatures and boardwalk amusements, a whole cosmos of stars. The boy next to her is drawing volcanoes and craters and little green men.

"My mama is a moon maiden," he announces.

The Mermother leaves the youngsters to their work and retreats to the observatory. A disturbance on the surface tells her that the ship is back, the squat little waterbug with the unhappy name, Miasma. The marine presence that makes the children hold their noses and squirm uneasily.

Must I rescue them all? she wonders. She pulls the net from the empty shell where she has hidden it and begins weaving again.

It is risky, she thinks, sending the boy into enemy territory. But how else will he learn that the World of Tomorrow need not be a threat?

She can feel progress, as sure as the tide. But there is more to be done. Coney Island cannot sustain itself on the past. The boy must bring back the future. And he must be the link that completes that circle of solidarity, that ring around Luna.

He will travel to the World's Fair in three days – just in time.Late daylight is spilling through the hatch where there once was a telescope, and the Mermother glances up at the reflections filtering through the opening. She is used to views of *cloudy weather, lonely figures, yawns, shrugs of resignation. She's grown accustomed to scenes of households in despair – angry mothers, humiliated fathers, unhappy children. Lately, these familiar portraits have been joined by that pest, the Funny Face. And also by ghostlike specters of something she's not seen in many years: armies forming on distant battlefields; feature-less men woken by war-cries; whole communities on the move, pursued by dust, tanks, and soldiers.*

But none of these grim images are present now. Instead, the Mermother is surprised to see a curious young face hovering at the surface. It is the face of a clever girl with strawberry blonde hair. She wears an expression of deep skepticism as she peers into the water at the end of the Dreamland Pier.

The Mermother catches her breath. The girl cannot see her, but she can very easily make herself seen – for this is the other Incubator Baby, Paloma Bright. And babies saved by the light of the night see easily through the dark of the day.

But she does not reveal herself. Paloma's loyalty will pass its own test. Instead, the Mermother shifts her gaze further down the beach to the man who has buried his handsome face in his hands. He, too, has made a net.

It will be okay, she tells herself. The boy has all he needs.

He has a doubting friend, a flailing hero, and an inventor with a ticket to the future.

CHAPTER TWENTY-FIVE

Paloma stands on the overground subway platform feeling more confused than she likes to admit. Ever since Buff sprinted up her stairs with the news that Doc wanted to take them to the World's Fair for the Fourth of July, she has felt like a ping-pong ball, bouncing between secret desires and fierce loyalties.

Now the day has come. The World of Tomorrow is just a subway ride away.

From the elevated platform she has a commanding view of Surf Avenue, sadly depopulated in spite of the holiday. A sorry pack of folks from the neighborhood is milling about the entrance of Luna Park, waiting in vain for signs of a parade.

Paloma is glad not to be the bearer of sad news – that there will be no Fourth of July Parade on Coney Island this year because the Commissioner refused to sign the permit.

"Who needs a stinkin' permit?" she had demanded when she heard the news, and she quickly embarked on a campaign to organize a homegrown parade. But even Myrtle Crespi, that prima donna, had declined. "We got more important things to build than parade floats," she had said importantly. And then she took Paloma by the hand and showed her what was happening in the Sideshow's back lot.

For the rest of the afternoon, Paloma watched Henry and Clyde busily building and dismantling, building and dismantling. There was arguing and then cheers, cheers and then arguing. Paloma pitched in—fetching nails, ropes, coffee and chalk—but she wasn't convinced that their combined efforts were any less bumbling than those of the dwarf clowns who rush about putting out miniature fires in Luna Park's Lilliputian Land. She was glad (and momentarily chastened) to learn that Henry was building a kid-catcher-catcher, and not, as she had previously suspected, a kid-catcher. But watching him at work felt dangerously like watching a lost cause.

Which is why Paloma is glad she has somewhere else to be today.

The World's Fair! She does a little jig of anticipation. Then she scolds herself. The Commissioner, after all, is Coney Island's sworn foe. Everyone knows that. And his mightiest weapon is the World of Tomorrow. She scowls and folds her arm across her chest to keep them still.

By the time Doc and Buff join her on the platform, Paloma Bright has hardened back into a stalwart Coney Island loyalist.

"I'm only going along as an observer," she states snootily. "Any true American worth his red white and blue blood knows that you celebrate the Fourth of July at Coney Island, not at some yippy-skippy World's Fair full of foreigners.

"Paloma," starts Buff, embarrassed at the implication. "Immigrants ain't foreigners."

"It's quite all right," interrupts Doc, fussing for subway fare in his change purse, "Paloma is just regarding our outing like a true social scholar. I avait your important observations. Perhaps you even have brought pencil and paper? Hm?"

The train arrives and Doc herds the children into the last car. He sits down on the bench across from them and folds his hands over his belly. "Vake me ven ve arrive, please," he says and is instantly whistle-snoring.

Paloma turns to Buff. "So?" she says

"So?"

"So what's new with the egg?"

Though there are only a few other riders in the car, Buff lowers his voice. "I can feel it changing. All the time. One minute it's sending out sparks and the next, it's sucking everything up – sounds, thoughts, even ideas."

Paloma doesn't say so, but she has felt it herself. For a seemingly inanimate object, the weird thing in the bassinet has a very animated presence. Just yesterday when she stopped by to visit Buff in the Incubator House, she saw Brigitte, the pretty junior nurse who keeps gumdrops in her apron pocket, standing next to the bassinet, overcome by giggles. Breddy had to send her home, she got such a bad case of hiccups.

"How about you?" asks Buff. "Any news from Ramsey? Henry?"

"Henry's a man on a mission and Ramsey's out to lunch. Neither of them seem like they're gonna crack a missing kids case, Buff."

Buff sighs. He pulls a newspaper clipping from his pocket and hands it to her. She unfolds it and reads: Parks Commissioner to Kick off Independence Day Festivities with Civic Exhortation at the World's Fair.

"Civic exhortation!" she sneers. "Sounds like something you don't wanna get at the doctor's office."

"Maybe it's time to concede a little. Meet the Commissioner halfway. Give him the baby exhibit in exchange for some help policing the boardwalk."

"Buff! You'd be hung from the Wonder Wheel for such thoughts!" exclaims Paloma with exaggerated horror. But her face changes quickly. "Golly! Do you think maybe the Commissioner's heard about it?"

"About what – the disappearances?"

"No. The egg, dummy. Maybe the whole offer to bring the babies is just a ploy to get the egg."

Buff thinks about this. Somehow he can't make the worlds of the Commissioner and his mermaid meet. But he's glad that the egg is safe in the Incubator Baby House with Breddy watching it around the clock.

"Because it could maybe be real valuable," explains Paloma. "It might be a rare albino elephant egg and the Commissioner wants it for his Fair."

"Elephants are mammals, Paloma. Like dolphins. They don't lay eggs."

"Which is why it's so rare!" she retorts.

"I dunno," shrugs Buff. "But I'm sure there are clues to be had at the Fair. They might be as important as the ones we found in the warehouse. More important even…"

He is about to say more, but he swallows the words. He's not sure how to tell Paloma to his theory: that he was running out of stories and Coney Island was running out of hope. And that maybe, just maybe, there was more to be found in the World of Tomorrow.

"It's just …" Buff starts to explain.

"Spit it out," says Paloma.

Buff looks out the window at the last of Luna's faded whirligigs disappearing.

"It's just that … I was given a message, whether you believe it or not. And that message was that to save Coney Island, we have to give it something new. We can't just freeze it in a point in time like a fossil. Coney is something to be created. Not preserved. And if everything in the World of Tomorrow is brand new…"

"Is that what your fish-lady says?" asks Paloma with a smirk. "What a nutter."

Buff takes the newspaper clipping and tucks it back in his pocket. Brooklyn clatters along unnoticed out the window.

"I took a gander, you know," says Paloma after a time. "Didn't see a bloomin' thing down there."

Buff doesn't answer. But he knows that when Paloma says she didn't see a sign of a mermaid at the end of the Dreamland Pier, what she means is – that she went looking for one. What she has just said is that she wants to believe him. That she has even gone looking for a reason to believe him.

What Buff doesn't know is that when she did, Paloma was struck by how difficult it was to clamber over the ruined pier and how frightening the dark water was at its end. She was struck, at the time, by how brave Buff has become.

Now Paloma studies her friend's face. Maybe he's right, she thinks. Maybe all this time her attempts to collect Coney Island in treasure boxes under the bed were not enough. Maybe she would have done better to leave those relics of the past in the weeds under the boardwalk, where they could grow into something new and unrecognizable.

"I asked Myrtle to check in on it today, while you're not there," she says softly. "Myrtle can talk a blue streak, you know."

Buff smiles. He is sure now. Paloma wants to believe him.

"Thanks."

Paloma turns to look out the window at the solid gray mass they are leaving behind.

"Looks like rain," she says.

But ahead, the sky above Queens is cloudless and blue.

Chapter Twenty-Six

The World's Fair that spreads itself before the Coney Island visitors when they pass through its Flushing Meadows Gate is overwhelming. As far as the eye can see, swarms of pedestrians, trolleys, dancers, parades and delegations fill the walks and lawns. The Fairground's vast expanse reminds Buff of a grass-green ocean. Stucco buildings rise gleaming and bright, like an army of whitecaps. Hundreds of miles of benches provide front-row seats to a spectacle in motion. The air hums of activity.

As Doc, Buff and Paloma gape on the sidelines, a marching band stomps past. The musicians are dressed in the green livery of New York City's Sanitation Brigade, and the drum section is made up of garbage bin lids. At the head, high-stepping and twirling a baton, is a short fat man with a double chin, a sweaty face, and an abundance of energy.

"Hey! You're my mayor!" hollers Paloma in recognition, and the Mayor of New York tosses her a carnation fashioned out of newspaper. "C'mon - let's see this Fair!" she exclaims, grabbing her companions by the hand.

Doc picks up a map from a nearby information stand. He hands it to Buff, who studies it as Paloma spins like a weather-vane in restless wind. "Communications Corridor … Automotive Annex … Fashion and Haberdashery … Oil and Gas. What the heck kinda funhouses are these?"

"Funhouses of the future, of course," says Doc. "Where to first?"

The morning passes quickly. Roaming the Plaza of Power and the Concourse of Commerce, the threesome have no choice but to acknowledge a certain magnificence to this immodest Fair of the Commissioner's. Magnificence that, at times, borders on intimidation. The Edison Court, they discover, echoes tremendously; the Refrigeration Foyer is unnaturally spotless; and the shadows looming in the corners of the windowless Westing House of Wares are even longer than the massive columns at its entrance.

Everywhere they go, Buff squints his eyes as if trying to find a missing link.

Everywhere they leave, Paloma acknowledges with a backward wave and the conclusion, "How 'bout that, Doc?"

Martin Couney, for his part, is silently imagining the possibilities of collaboration in this World's Fair, where his neighbors would be captains of industry and titans of technology, not captains of canoe rides and turners of teacup rides.

There are endless attractions to visit and demonstrations to watch. When the Sonic Cannon in the Timepiece Terminal booms twelve times for noon, they have covered just a fraction of the Fair. Buff makes a mental tally: three talking robots, an electric farm, seven synchronized fountains and four motorized bicycle contraptions.

When they reach the Plaza of Nations, Doc insists on a short "sittensiedown." Paloma starts a running commentary on the live models in the traditional dress of their homelands.

"By golly that's a big bonnet for little gal," she says of a tyke in an elaborate peasant hat. "Yikes! The ruffle on that thing alone could dress me!" she says of a woman dancing a Sevillana down the path. She gives a low whistle of approval for Cossacks bristling with daggers, Mexican gauchos in sequins and delicate women sheathed in exotic silks of the Far East. For the Dutch boy in wooden shoes, she has a hearty laugh. "Don't cross the mob with those on, boy-o, or you'll have done half their job for them!" Cooing over the ribbons and fanciful headwear of a young woman with cheeks the color of macintosh apples, Paloma notes, "I'm not sure they belong in the World of Tomorrow, though." Doc, who knows these Old World dress styles well, frowns. "I fear that you may be right," he says, with a sad glance at Miss Czechoslovakia.

It is after two o'clock when Doc suggests lunch. Buff

and Paloma look at the old man with a look that says Lunch? There are highways of the future to drive and three-dimensional films to watch and a giant human ear to crawl through! There are stunt men rappelling from the Trylon and Peruvian parrots in the July Jungle! But then a waft of vegetable soup rolls out of the nearby Canned Goods Café, and the kids agree to lunch.

When Doc has mopped up the last of his soup with a piece of brown bread and licked his spoon clean, he leans back in his chair and gazes contentedly up at the centerpiece of the open cafeteria. It is a giant column filled with water and goldfish. At its top, higher than most diners bother to look, is a gold-plated figure of a woman holding an egg. Doc raises his eyebrows with interest but does not point it out to his young companions.

Instead, he leans back across the table and steals a handful of Paloma's oyster crackers.

"Now, Buff," he says. "Tell me vat important insights you have gathered from dis future world. And tell me, too, vat it is you sink to hear from the Commissioner on de matter of Independence in the Future. For I am of a mind dat such a topic is, as dey say, not avoidable given our particular time and place today."

Buff wipes his mouth carefully and puts his napkin under the soup bowl.

"Well, this is an awfully interesting Fair, that's for sure. Inspirational too. But there's not a lot of imagination."

"No imagination? Mit electric cows and rubber balls as big as my head? No imagination?"

"I guess maybe I mean the magical imagination," Buff clarifies. "Not the scientific kind of imagination."

"Ahh." The inventor of the incubator raises his eyes again to the top of the column – to the valiant woman and her egg presiding over the chattering diners below. He feels humbled. Such a vast planet. Its population ever increasing, despite all of man's actions to impede it. Silently, he counts up the babies who have come in and out of his life over the decades. Most of them, he hopes, will live to a ripe old age. But he, their lifesaver, needs no gold-plated statue.

"You know dat I have been invited to bring the babies to the Fair, ja?" he asks.

Buff nods. "I think you should do it." He ignores Paloma, who is looking at him as if he has grown a second head, and continues: "I don't know that you need the Fair, Doc. But this Fair needs you. It needs the Incubators."

Doc raises his eyebrows and leans forward, placing his elbow directly in a puddle of soup.

"Everything here is so sure that it's brand spanking new, it's as if maybe we've all forgotten that every day is new," Buff continues.

Doc nods at this modest wisdom but says nothing.

"Plus – this idea that you can plan the future and make it perfect ... Well, what about the things that don't come out so perfect? They still have a place in the world, right?" argues Buff. "You don't reject them ... just like you don't let premature babies die. There needs to be a place for your kind of science, or innovation, or imagination, or whatever. A place that doesn't make things perfect, but makes imperfect things ... okay."

"I sink you are saying dat the magic we see here today, de magic of Progress, it still needs de glow of Mother Nature's magic, ja?"

Paloma swallows the chocolate milk she has been holding in her mouth since the beginning of the conversation and speaks. "We still haven't been to see the actual World of Tomorrow," she says, pointing to the giant globe, the Perisphere, in the center of the map.

"Vell, such a visit was never in question," agrees Doc Couney, folding his napkin. "De big ball, it is de center of gravity, nein? So wipe your mouth-es and finish your milks and off ve go to de center of de Future."

CHAPTER TWENTY-SEVEN

They are on their way to the Perisphere when Doc Couney stops at the intersection of two broad avenues. He points to an elegant façade with glass doors, all covered in posters: **NEW ATTRACTION COMING SOON.**

"Dat's vere dey want me to bring the babies."

Buff and Paloma run up the wide stairs to the entry and peer through the slits between the posters. The interior of the empty building is easily five times the size of Luna Park's Incubator Baby House. It is a vast semicircular arena ringed with a high balcony. Dust motes swim in the sunlight pouring in from small oval windows near the ceiling.

"Like portholes in a ship," says Paloma.

"Imagine how teeny the babies would seem from all the way up there," says Buff. He is looking at the far wall, where the faded outline of an eagle with outstretched wings is still visible. The bird, it appears, held a crooked cross in its talons.

A tall shadow crawls up the children's backs and strong hands grasp them by their collars. "This building is not open to the public," says a voice bristling with irritation. Buff squirms to view the body behind the hands and bites his tongue painfully. Paloma squeaks in surprise at the face reflected in the glass.

"But I sink perhaps it is open to me." Doc's welcome voice from behind loosens the Commissioner's grasp slightly. "I am Martin Couney," he says, huffing slightly from the trot he has broken into. "I believe dat you are hoping to see more of me. And of my ... hmm, children."

The Commissioner releases Buff and Paloma and straightens to his full height. He extends a hand to the doctor and says it's a pleasure to meet him, though neither Buff nor Paloma believes it's true. They are impressed by the man's commanding presence. It has made them feel very small and very quiet. Neither of them recalls wanting to ask him questions.

"My people tell me that you are still undecided, Dr. Couney, about whether or not to accept our invitation to display your neonatal incubation model at the Fair," says the Commissioner without a smile. "As you have no doubt witnessed if you have spent any time at all here today, indecision is not generally something we promote. If you have any questions about the facilities or the financing we can provide you as an exhibitor, please do ask. I'm afraid I have very little time. I am due at the Trylon Grandstand shortly, you see. I have a speech to give."

The Commissioner taps his foot.

"Vell. It's very kind of you to take a personal interest," says Doc. He pulls a handkerchief from his pocket and begins polishing his glasses like a man with plenty of time to chat. "I would like to introduce you to my companions here."

The Commissioner glances at his wristwatch.

"Dis is Buff and dis is Paloma. They are both having some influence in, as dey say, hardening my convictions."

The Commissioner gives the slightest of nods to the children, noting as he does, that the boy is looking at him with the intensity of a biologist mid-way through a dissection. He touches his abdomen, overwhelmed by the fleeting notion that he has become a splayed frog.

"Ve have learned a great deal from our exploration today," continues the old man amiably. "Vat did you say to me, Buff? About dat ingenious waterfall tunnel we passed into de whatsit – Power Grid? Ah yes, you said 'power is always safest when evenly dispersed.' Perfectly sound scientific understanding of electricity, nein?

"Und Paloma here, she too has made interesting observations. Ja, she is very keen on de young people you have walking about in the get-ups of the flags of the world. De

World of Tomorrow flags – dey are so much like de flags of today, so dat is, I sink, a most reassuring costume. But my Paloma noticed, particularly, de un-comfort of some of the boys and girls representing our own great nation on the Plaza of Nations. She said to me, 'Ain't nussink hotter than a suit of stars and stripes on a hot day in July!' Ha! A good one, no?"

Doc's chuckle is not shared by the Commissioner.

"Yes, well. We take pride in elevating this World's Fair to the true meaning of the name," he says. "And I think you will agree that it is particularly important to demonstrate the humanity of all our allies abroad. We must fight nationalism and socialism with humanism."

"Ah yes. By dressing our humans up as nations and making dem wave, social-like. I see, clever." Doc nods seriously. "I am, as you know…"

"German. Yes I know. Which is why it is appropriate that you occupy this…"

"I am German, yes, in fact," interrupts the doctor. "Which is why it is appropriate that I not occupy anything. I leave dis occupying to bullies like the de Chancellor dat was originally invited to display his own convictions in this dis fine Pavilion."

Buff and Paloma stand utterly still, transfixed by the exchange. In the distance a band strikes up a lively round of "American Patrol." Suddenly the Commissioner turns and addresses Buff.

"Do you not take pride in being a New Yorker on a day like today, young man? Is there any better place to celebrate our nation, its position in the global society, and its dedication to liberty, peace and freedom?"

Buff swallows painfully.

"I, I... do. I do... take pride," he stammers. "This is a very fine Fair, Mr. Commissioner. And if what you mean by liberty is the freedom to build your own future – well, sir, I, um, I hope that your Fair inspires people everywhere, in all places to dedicate themselves to it and even to...to fight for it."

Buff looks up to make eye contact with the Commissioner, but he balks at the coldness he finds there.

"That way," he continues, his eyes now fixed behind the man, on the gleaming spire of the Trylon pinned against the sky, "when the Fair is gone, there will be plenty of places all over New York ... and all over the world, where people can celebrate ...whatever they choose to celebrate. Liberty or, you know, lesser blessings. In any way they choose to celebrate." Buff pauses, distracted momentarily by the sight of clouds forming low on the southern horizon. Then he lifts his eyes once more to the Commissioner and boldly presses his conclusion: "Without rules about how. Without regulations about where."

The Commissioner's silence seems stunned. He is

used to accusations; he has many enemies in the halls of New York's politics, and not a day goes by when a fist isn't waved at him. But this is the first time he has flinched. The Commissioner's legendary thick skin feels very thin.

From the main path, a nervous voice: "Mr. Commissioner, sir. It's time."

"I must be going, Doctor Couney," says the Commissioner brusquely, turning on his heel. But before he has reached the steps of the empty Pavilion, he pivots again and returns. Not to Doc, but to Buff. He squats before the boy so he can look him in the eye.

"I am not a tyrant, son," he says. "I am a servant. I serve my city. I serve my country. I serve my conscience."

He rises and addresses Doc once more: "I am a man of action. I apologize if we have misunderstood each other, Doctor Couney. But I must warn you. You should not stall for time. The opportunity I am providing for you here is more than a reward for your good work. It is an exit plan. It is time for you to leave Luna Park. Coney Island is dead."

With that, he is gone, brushing aside his waiting entourage with a single wave of his hand.

"What did he mean – 'stalling for time'," asks Paloma.

"He means vaiting for nature to take its course. Which is vat ve do in an incubator ward. And, what we have always done on Coney Island."

216

Doc looks at Buff. "I believe you impressed him more dan I did, Buff."

Buff is watching the Parks Commissioner striding down his fairgrounds, parting the crowd like a plough. He is thinking about his egg. He's sucking his sore tongue. Whatever hint of respectful curiosity he had felt for the powerful figure is gone, replaced by the recognition of a common bully.

"I don't need to hear that man's speech," he says.

Chapter Twenty-Eight

Mingus Lamont stands on a dock in the weedy shallows of Flushing Bay, a ten-minute walk from the building where the Commissioner and Buff have just had their exchange. He has come up the river from Brooklyn. He bears a small delivery and big news for his powerful patron. He looks over his shoulder at the ugly little cargo boat and cackles at the seasick ruffian staggering over its rail.

"Get a move on, ya big lummox," he yells. The boy groans and clutches his empty belly.

Mingus Lamont marches down the dock to a truck path where a fat man with a three-day-old beard and frayed trousers is leaning against a van. The van, which until recently was used to transport slabs of beef from the slaughterhouse to market, stands with its back end open. Flies buzz nostalgically around the open door.

Lamont pulls an envelope from his jacket. "This here's for this load and for another later tonight. It's gonna be a special delivery, that one. I'll be in charge of unloading, all I need is your vehicle and your tight lips. You got it?"

The fat man pulls a toothpick from his mouth and says tiredly, "I got no idea what you're talkin' about, Mister."

"Perfect," says Mingus Lamont and rubs his hands gleefully. "Now get busy unloading. There's seven crates of American flags in there and seven more of wieners. I want them all delivered to the warehouse behind the Telephony Theater. Got it?"

The man re-inserts his toothpick and swats at the fly resting on the tip of his nose. It's as close as he comes to acknowledgement.

"Lou, ya dumb monkey," yells Lamont to the green-faced goon. "I'll meet you back here in an hour. I got some bizness up at the fairgrounds."

Lou just groans again and covers his pallor with a Funny Face mask.

The Trylon is reflecting late sun off its spine when Mingus Lamont arrives at the center of the fairgrounds. He glances at the darkening band to the south that signals storm clouds coming up from Brooklyn. He checks his watch, scratches his head and mutters something about the tide and the lack of light. Then he hangs a left at the Avenue of Peace and heads for the Theater of Telephonics, where the Commissioner keeps his World's Fair office.

Lamont is pleased with himself. The mousy woman from Yonkers had accepted his invitation and arrived with her unfortunate orphans this morning, prepared for a whole day of amusement at the Pavilion of Fun, compliments of the manager himself. "It will be a day they won't soon remember ...er, forget," promised Lamont. "A holiday that will simply transport those poor kiddoes, ma'am. That I can guarantee."

Now, he fairly skips with the thought of his coming triumph. "Nail in the coffin," he chortles. "Wait till those Coney die-hards get a load of Mingus Lamont, Deputy Parks Commissioner."

Cocky and crafty, Lamont scarcely notices the surging crowds around him. He is too busy imagining the filet mignon and lobster Newburgh that he and the Commissioner will be dining on after his official swearing-in. He glances once more at the horizon and counts the hours.

Barging through the lines of fairgoers waiting for a first-ever chance to place an international telephone call, Lamont knocks on the door of the antechamber leading to the Commissioner's office. It is opened by the man himself. The Commissioner, gripping a black binder in one hand and a set of keys in the other, pulls up short. Distaste is evident on his stony face.

"Just a minute of your time, yer estimable-ness," begins Mingus Lamont.

"I'm in a hurry," snaps the Commissioner as he locks the door behind him. "I have a speech to give."

"Just a second then," hurries Lamont. "I just came to report that your wishes, as far as that 'last nail' business goes, are being taken care of as we speak, sir."

The Commissioner, still bothered by his encounter with a grey-eyed thirteen-year-old, is walking quickly through the Telephonics Theater. The cavernous space rings and buzzes with dozens of long-distance conversations and busy switchboards. Dimly, he hears a woman's excited voice as she grips the handpiece: "Mamachka, is that you? I'm calling from the World's Fair! Mamachka, did I wake you? Mamachka, will you come to America? It's safer here, peaceful, Mamachka...."

Lamont, the Commissioner realizes, is sticking to his heels like a dog's mess. He tries to focus on what the little man is saying: "Yes indeed. Two dozen specimens, delivery set for midnight tonight."

The Commissioner pushes open a side door and the two men step into sunlight and a circle of assistants anxious to get their boss to the Trylon Grandstand.

"I thought, you know, you could announce the break in the case tomorrow. Grab another spin around the news cycle. Cap your Independence Day celebration nicely," Lamont is saying. "Symbolic, like." He pauses, waiting for the Commissioner to ask for details or dole out praise. But there is only silence.

"At any rate," continues Lamont, scratching his neck,

which has grown itchy under the Commissioner's glower. "The, er, transaction is in good hands. I will be taking personal delivery shortly and overseeing transport. All you need to do, sir, is be ready to, er, state the obvious when it arrives. You know, 'the fate of our young generation and the safety of our great city' and – well – I don't need to tell you what to say."

"No," says the Commissioner finally. "You certainly do not, Mr. Lamont. That will be all."

Lamont shudders slightly at the chill in the Commissioner's voice. He gives an uncomfortable snort and follows it with an awkward bow. The Commissioner watches him scuttle away and feels fresh anger rise in his chest. He directs it south — an unflinching arrow aimed at Coney Island. He scowls at the sound of a rogue tuba and wonders why his celebratory day has turned so dark. The face of the boy – Doctor Couney's boy – flashes before him and he touches his abdomen tenderly, feeling for the gaping wound.

The Commissioner starts for his waiting car. As he does, he stumbles on a paving stone and curses angrily. "Why is this block unsecured? Why! This is an unacceptable breach of the level walkway!" He kicks the dislodged stone with such force it flies, airborne, directly into a nearby aqualon. The stone shatters the glass, spilling water onto the path. Five goldfish flop helplessly on the pavement. A groundskeeper appears from nowhere and scrambles to scoop them up, but he freezes at the commanding voice: "Leave them! Leave them to reap the consequences of their idleness. Leave them to suffer the fate of stupid beasts of inaction! I will not tolerate swimming in circles, will not tolerate purposeless baubles! Leave them, I say!"

As the groundskeeper beats a hasty retreat, the Commissioner grips the binder that holds his Independence Day speech tightly. Somewhere in its pages is the declaration of the successful conclusion of a grand plan to rehabilitate the city and restore faith in the strength of the nation. But the Commissioner can only hear the nasal voice of Mingus Lamont: you can announce the successful resolution…conclusion…the last nail … and a sudden shock of panic replaces his anger.

The Commissioner looks back at the spot where he dismissed the crooked carny, but Lamont is gone. He looks down at the ground, where all but two of the goldfish have stopped gasping for waterless air. He looks at his entourage of aides, who have turned their faces away from his outburst. He takes a deep breath and buries his anxiety.

"I never ordered nails from that man," he says sourly.

Then the Parks Commissioner climbs into the back seat of his long black car and banishes all thoughts of Coney Island and its lazy, purposeless inhabitants.

Back in Coney Island, the Funny Face gang has its hands full. There is no shortage of youngsters in the park today, thanks to the holiday and the distracted lady from Yonkers.

At first, it seemed that the headmistress of the foundlings' home was going to be a nuisance. As soon as she climbed down from the rattly bus and laid eyes on Lamont's personal envoy, she proved to be a sourpuss, declining his offer to be the group's personal guide. Within fifteen minutes the boy named Bugs had arranged for the headmistress's glasses to be plucked from her nose while riding the Circuit Breaker and then trampled under foot.

"A gazillion apologies, ma'am," he said sorrowfully, holding the snapped spectacles. "I'll get these fixed in a jiffy. In the meantime, please accept dese here movie tickets as a token."

"A token," she repeated.

"Yeah."

"A token of what?"

"Of a double feature," Bugs answered, rolling his eyes impatiently.

"But I can't see."

"Lady – it's a big screen," he said in exasperation.

In the end, Bugs escorted the stubborn old biddy by the elbow across the road to the movie theater. Even bought her a tub of popcorn. The last thing she said as he left her in the dark was: "You'll take good care of them? Won't let them leave your sight?"

"Not a chance," he sneered as he shuffled back out of the theater.

But now he is having a hard time keeping his word.

"The heck they feed them up in Yonkers?" he wonders aloud as he grabs a hyperactive redhead for the fourth time and drags him off towards the warehouse. "BEANS!" hollers the boy, twisting out of his grasp to run and hide in the Magic Barrel.

"They thinks it's a doggone game," hollers another pimply-faced delinquent, pushing up his mask just in time to see the girl he has just collared run back into the Pavilion of Fun, shrieking with laughter. "It's like herding cats," he says and drops to the ground in fatigue.

Another masked Funny Face is rubbing his shin where one of the orphans had given him a solid kick. "Mingus don't pay enough for this," he whines. "I mean it's one thing to keep 'em locked in the pen till he brings the boat back. But we gotta catch the brats first. And that ain't no joke."

Bugs taps his head hard, trying to knock just one more good idea out of it before the sun starts to set.

"They wanna play a game?" he says. "Let's give 'em a game."

"What game is that, Bugs?"

"It's called 'Last one in is a rotten egg.'"

And in no time at all, the shack in the Steeplechase warehouse is full of children all reconsidering the merits of being a rotten egg.

CHAPTER TWENTY-NINE

The sun is setting on Coney Island when Myrtle Crespi decides she's had enough of the Incubator Baby House. She has been in the ward for close to an hour, a fish out of water among the tidy nurses with their crisp uniforms and soothing voices. All this time, Myrtle has tried to rise to Paloma's challenge – to tell a whopper of a story, "one that could crack an egg." But Myrtle has come up uncharacteristically empty. She has tried everything – including giving the strange orb an imaginary mustache, twinkling eyes and diamond cufflinks – but it hasn't made her any chattier. Now she cocks her head and squints suspiciously at the bassinet. The thing inside it has turned pinkish, and Myrtle thinks maybe it's making fun.

"The heck am I doing here?" she says, rising to go.

Just then the senior nurse appears at her side. "Leaving, Miss Crespi?" she asks. "There's another storm brewing. Have you got an umbrella?"

Breddy's approach has given the other nurses an excuse to get a longer look at the odd visitor. They eye Myrtle's rumpled chiffon dress and her lace-up gladiator sandals with curiosity. They consider her loud red hair. They count the silver bangles on her arm with envy. Myrtle glares back, sending them scurrying about their business. "I move too fast for the rain," she says.

Breddy smiles. "Well, it was good of you to come. I know Buff was worried about leaving it…" She jerks her head at the bassinet.

"It's a pretty bauble, whatever it is," says Myrtle.

"Yes. Whatever it is."

Myrtle touches the glimmering egg once more. It feels like melting ice and crumbling coal. When she looks up again, she sees that the nurse is looking at her, and not at the egg. Breddy opens her mouth and then closes it. She clears her throat, wrinkles her brow and starts again: "I believe I see the kiss of Couney on you, Miss."

"Beg pardon?" asks Myrtle, startled.

"Buff and Paloma were among my first babies," says Breddy. "I'm sure you were already a young lady when I came to work for the Doctor. Still, you can tell when a person's cheated death. And you, Miss Crespi, have that look."

Myrtle sits back heavily in the chair and stares at the nurse. Years of caring for babies have given Breddy a wrap of maturity, but Myrtle can see that the nurse is not many years older than she is her-self. If Doc Couney has never recognized Myrtle for the baby she once was, how, she wonders, has this woman? She is silent for a minute, searching for a smart retort for the nosy busy-body. But she doesn't have one. All she has is this an old secret. And now, for the first time in her life, Myrtle thinks she wants it told. It is, after all, a whopper of a story.

"I was born in Manhattan, just a few hours after my ma got distracted on Essex Street and let herself get run down by a bus," she begins.

"The doctor had a hard time getting me clear of all the mess, but when he did, he wrapped my three pounds of bones in a blanket, called up Luna 6-5-1, and said 'Couney – I've got a tenant for you.' They brought me down pronto. But when I got to Luna Park, the cribs were all full. So the Doctor comes out and he points down Surf Avenue to where he had set up his second Baby House - brand-spanking new in a brand-new Park, Coney's new-est attraction. A fantasy land not to be believed. Heav-en on Earth and the Garden of Eden with a peek at the Underworld thrown in. At least, that was what it was supposed to be. That was the dream. But, well…not all dreams are meant to be, dontcha know."

"Dreamland," says Breddy, understanding. "Oh…"

"Yup. I got there the night before opening day. And

they're still working all over the park, getting ready, burning the midnight oil, so to speak. On the far side of the park, all manner of animals – prowling their cages, 'cause they smell the scent of a disaster coming on."

"It was 1911," says Breddy.

"You betcha it was," answers Myrtle. "May 27, 1911. Eight hours till Dreamland opens for its debut season. Deep down in the bowels of the park, a handful of workmen are putting the last touches on a dark ride called Hell Gate. And down there in Hell Gate, some fella gets careless with his lantern and a bucket of pitch. They get too close, and they make a hiss and a pop, and within three minutes Hell is on fire."

The ward has fallen unusually silent. Myrtle hears her own hush. She hears the silence of the Incubator Babies in their Dreamland cribs twenty-eight years and a whole lifetime ago.

"So there I was," she says. "Pumping my fist, 'cause I had made it that far. But that too, was premature on my part. Cause all us babies were back at square one, if you know what I mean.

"The fire spread faster than any mechanical ride at Coney," she continues, her story rushing to catch up with the flames. "It roared out the caverns of Hell Gate and raced along the souvenir stands until it reached the puppet theaters. The strung-up marionettes danced a conga when their cat-gut strings snapped in the heat. All around them, the Alps of Bavaria and the Dunes of Sahara and the Tulips of the Tuileries zoomed upward in a cyclone of cinders. The flames let loose, cruising crazy through the promenades, eating up the buildings like so much cotton candy. Up in smoke went the Oriental Bazaar! The Octopus Tank bubbled and boiled! The fire found the barrels of popping corn and they exploded just like gunpowder and filled the walks with great white tumbleweeds ... the elephants took one look at this gi-nor-mous-met-a-morph-osis of their favorite treat and started trumpeting; but I'll tell you sister, they ran from it like the abomination it was! There were monkeys jimmying up stage curtains just seconds ahead of the flames, dancing along power lines, hot-stepping it over the exploding bulbs. In the main electrical control house, the chief engineer threw the power main, trapping the park in darkness... until the fire raged higher."

Myrtle catches her breath and wiggles in her chair. Breddy leans closer. Four young nurses are frozen in their tracks, transfixed.

"Now, it was just six minutes after the fire began that Miss Graf, (that was the name of the lady who had your job), felt her nose itching with smoke. She rounded up her nurses and assigned each a pair of infants. They soaked the blankets in water from the tap, wrapped up the babies and plunged headlong into the fire, somehow making it unburnt to Surf Avenue.

"Cacophony and chaos outside! Four fire engines pulled by six horses apiece charging in from Ocean Parkway! And the firefighters spilled out onto the street by the dozen! They were brave men in their muscle shirts and hard hats and they made for the west gate. But just as they were getting ready to scale the wall, they were met by all the little people of Lilliputia rushing to escape their flaming miniature village. So they haul out the trampolines and forty-three midgets bounce to safety.

"The minutes pass and already it was clear – there wasn't gonna be much to save of Dreamland." Myrtle lets her voice drop into a dramatic dirge. "A mariachi band in sequined sombreros struck up a song – and Dreamland's central tower collapsed to the tune of 'Juan Colorado.'"

Myrtle Crespi squeezes her eyes against the cataclysm of Dreamland, which is vivid in her awakened memories. Nurse Breddy steals a glance at the bassinet and is startled to see the reflection of flames in its glass top. She looks quickly to the ceiling — there is nothing but the dusty overhead lamps.

"In the end, what it came down to was this …" continues Myrtle. "Exactly the sensation the men who dreamed up Dreamland had dreamed of. A double-nine-alarm fire, with two hundred firemen powerless to put it out! The shooting galleries—ripped open by their own live ammo! The street – filled with singed animals and rivers of melted ice cream! It was a pyrotechnic spectacular, a catastrophe, an adventure! It was everything Dreamland needed to be...except finished ...and in ashes."

"But you," interrupts Breddy. "You were saved."

Myrtle's eyes sparkle. "Out on Surf Avenue, that Nurse Graf huddled with her nurses and babies and began a headcount. There were four nurses and eight babies. One was missing. I'll give you three guesses who ..."

She holds her hands to the side of her face in mock alarm and yells, "'Ach! The one who came just tonight! The littlest baby, a baby girl! Left behind in the last crib!' That's what Nurse Graf told the fireman. And you know what that firefighter said? He said: 'It's too late for her, miss.'

"How do you like that? First too early, then too late. I mean, the deck was really stacked against me! Well, Nurse Graf collapsed right then and there, but then someone in the crowd points into the flames and yells 'What in heaven's name is that?'

"And I'll tell you what it was – it was the Rex the Lion King scaling the last standing wall of Dreamland, his mane ablaze. His eyes were sad, like he knows what's coming and he's ready to punch it once and lay down. And what else? In his great jaws...a small bundle of blanket.

"'My baby,' shrieked the nurse. And, true story — that Lion nodded his head to confirm it. Then he took a final leap over the circus tent as it blew its big top in a shower of sparks, and in mid-leap he sling-shotted that bundle that was mostly blanket and a little bit of baby so that it sailed over the inferno and went falling, falling right down into the nurse's open arms."

Myrtle is breathing heavily. There's a roar in her ears. Maybe it's the ghost of Rex or the ghost of fire, or maybe it's just the distant surf. But underneath it is a childish melody – *we all fall down, we all fall down.*

"And that's how I cheated death not just once, but twice," she concludes. "In one night. That is what you saw, Nurse Breddy, but what nobody else 'round here has ever put together. That is my kiss of Couney."

For a full minute, silence reigns in the Incubator Baby House. And then there is a single wail from one of the cribs. Breddy ignores it. She is staring at Myrtle in amazement.

"But why, Miss Crespi?" she asks. "Why have you never told anyone? Why have you not revealed yourself as the miracle you are?"

Myrtle shrugs. She doesn't know. "Ta-da," she says weakly, and then adds, "I guess now I can't very well claim to be a Rockefeller no more."

The nurse glances up at the visitor's gallery, which has

234

been empty all day. She is surprised to see a man standing there, staring blankly through the glass windows.

"We have a visitor," she says.

Myrtle looks up to see Handsome Henry, his face a wreck of sadness.

Chapter Thirty

Myrtle hurries up the ramp to the bally-man, who holds a stopwatch in one hand and a long rope in the other.

"Calculations musta been off," Henry says in a flat voice. "There's twenty-some kids missing from Steeplechase today. I've failed."

Myrtle covers her mouth in alarm, and then takes Henry's hands in hers. The rope drops to the floor.

"You did your best, Handsome," she says. "You ain't a superhero, after all."

"No. Not a superhero. Not a hero at all. A coward."

"Come on, now. Don't go beatin' yerself up. We just gotta get out there and find them is all."

Henry isn't looking at Myrtle as she reassures him. He is looking down at the Incubator ward and its cribs full of safety. Myrtle follows his gaze.

"At least those little ones aren't going nowhere," she says.

"I been avoiding this place for years," is Henry's answer.

"How come? The babies make you nervous?"

"No. Not the babies," he says. "It's the mothers."

Henry leans his forehead against the glass and sighs.

"I only came in one time before now. My first season on Coney. Came in with a girl to get outta the rain. I remember making a wisecrack about the fella at the ticket-booth outside. He was dressed in nappies and a bonnet. Then we came inside and that's when…"

"When what?" asks Myrtle after a long silence.

"I don't remember seeing any babies, you wanna know the truth," says Henry. "Don't remember any babies. I only remember the woman standing in the corner." Henry points with his hat to the far end of the gallery. "She was younger, I'm guessing, than she looked. Young, but it looked to me that she would never be young again. She was crying, but with no sound. Just her shoulders, her head, her hands. All crying softly. I knew she was here because she had lost one of her own. She was grieving for her lost baby."

Henry looks up and Myrtle sees tears in his eyes.

"Memory lane is one heckuva ride," she says, stroking his hand.

The bally-man grips her fingers tightly and speaks again. "That woman. She tore me all up. Shook me to the core. Because that woman … she could have been, she very well could have been…"

Myrtle squeezes back.

"She could have been my mother."

With that, the strong man with the sly detachment whom Myrtle has admired for so long, falls on her shoulder and buries his face in the explosion of her hair.

"Handsome?" she whispers, her voice betraying her surprise.

"I was twelve years old when my baby brother died," she hears him say. "When he died, my mother grew old. Overnight. So I did too. I told her I would take care of the others, but I didn't. After just a month, I left instead. I left because I couldn't stand seeing my mother. So old. So sad. So alone. Nothing I could say or do would make her happy. Or young. And I left. I left my mother alone with her sadness."

Myrtle waits.

"I left. I left my mother and my siblings behind. I ran away, Myrtle. And then I lost them. The dust storms were starting and forced them to leave home, too. They musta gone west when I went east. I have not heard from them since. I looked for them. Every winter I would start the hunt again – I looked for them everywhere, but there's no trace and it's because I ran away, Myrtle. Like a coward. And now I have to make it up to them. I have to return all those children to their mothers. I cannot leave them alone. We can't leave them alone in their sadness, Myrtle."

What Myrtle says in response is a whisper that no one but Henry hears.

But some time later, when Myrtle and Henry exit the Incubator Baby House hand in hand, the egg in the bassinet below rolls clear across its crib and issues a deep but unresolved crack.

It, too, has heard.

Sliver Moon
July 4, 1939

*T*he Mermother is startled by the sharp snap of a signal – it comes from the egg. Things are shifting on land.

"It begins," she murmurs. "Children, come close."

The Mermother pulls a clamshell from her belt and opens it to reveal white sand under a seafoam puff. She tickles each child's face with the puff, smoothing away the seasalt. Next she hands each boy a bow-tie made of seaweed and instructs them to help each other dress.

"We want to look our best when we arrive," she explains.

"Where we going?" asks Oscar.

The Mermother doesn't answer. She is combing Mary Lou's flaxen hair and listening.

CHAPTER THIRTY-ONE

Buff, Paloma and Doc Couney arrive at the Perisphere only to find that they are too late.

"The World of Tomorrow will reopen tomorrow," notes the girl in the ticket booth brightly.

"And the World of Tomorrow today? It is closed?" asks Doc. "Perhaps we are faced wid de place's inherent contrary-diction?"

"Oh. Well, I don't know about your heirs, and I can understand your accent just fine," says the ticket seller quizzically. "But you see, the Commissioner is delivering his Liberty Address. And we know that our guests don't want to miss that."

Doc ignores the snort from Paloma. He tips his hat.

"Most solicitous of you," he says as he herds the children away from the window.

"Well, don't that beat all," harrumphs Paloma as the threesome stand awkwardly in the middle of a crush of fairgoers hurrying towards the Trylon.

The public address system crackles in the overhead speakers: "All visitors make their way immediately to the

Trylon Grandstand for the much anticipated Liberty Address and Celebration of Fireworks."

Another chattering group of excited visitors round the corner, jostling the threesome from the path. Buff finds himself pushed up against an aqualon. As it happens, it is the only one of the decorative tanks in all the Fairgrounds that the grounds crew missed when they hurried to execute The Commissioner's orders. As a result, the aqualon is still lined with pebbles rather than sand. Buff kneels to get a closer look. He taps the glass, but the circling fish do not respond. Instead, he hears the voice of the mermaid: Fill it with the future.

Impulsively, Buff unscrews the top of the aqualon. He reaches into the water and plucks a single pebble from the bottom. The fish are undisturbed, but Buff's head is buzzing.

"Let's go home," he says, pocketing the pebble. "I think we've got all we need."

Doc turns and raises his eyebrows at this, but Paloma is distracted. She had insisted on trying every egg cream at the dairy farm and now she's regretting it.

"All I wanna do right now is find a bathroom," she says, jumping from foot to foot. "There!" she says pointing across the square to a small building with a sign reading COMFORT STATION. "I'll be right back!"

In an instant Paloma has disappeared amidst a fresh

onslaught of people hurrying for the grandstand. Doc, too, has been swallowed by the crowd. His voice remains: "Tactical retreat kiddos! We meet at the subway platform!"

Buff fights his way against the surge, like a salmon spawning upstream. He reaches the outer wall of the Perisphere and hugs it with his back, pulling his toes away from the trampling herd. After a moment the square clears enough to afford a glimpse of Doc Couney's hat bouncing towards the exit. He is just about to follow when, next to him, a double door opens and a large group exits the Perisphere. Without a thought, Buff slips into the closing doors of the World of Tomorrow.

When the doors slam shut behind him, Buff finds himself in low light. Extending his fingertips to touch the walls, he walks up a steep ramp towards an opening, a lightening. He walks for a long time, his shoes echoing in the near dark, and when he reaches the top of the ramp he feels the enormity of space around him. Buff is standing at a railing far above the Perisphere's equator. On the other side of the railing is a void. He looks over the railing gingerly and marvels at its pull. Far below, in the semi-darkness, he can make out an orderly grid suggesting boundaries, landforms, urban enclosures, rural expanses. He squints at the terraces and avenues and evenly spaced topography of the World of Tomorrow.

"Whatcha hiding from, future?" he says softly, but his

voice echoes all the same.

Suddenly, a row of klieg lights clank on and the land-scape below is illuminated by a thousand watts. Buff jumps in surprise. He looks around, expecting to see a guard on a watchtower manning a spotlight. But there is no sign of anyone else in the amphitheater. Buff is alone. His heart beating like a jackrabbit, Buff circles the arena, his left hand on the railing, the World of Tomorrow laid out below him. This is what he sees:

Canopied highways and soundless automobiles.

Sootless skyscrapers and pigeon-free plazas.

Patchwork quilts of farmland,

mountains scaled by funiculars,

rivers rushing to electrify the nation, and orchards of perfectly pruned trees.

He sees contentment and complacency. He sees a close brush with perfection.

Buff pauses in his circuit and peers down with more scrutiny. The figures below are moving, he sees now. The bicycles coasting downhill, but also gliding uphill. The farmers picking strawberries, but from bushes taller than trees. Tiny people turning in rotating doors but never, Buff can see, entering or exiting.

This is it? Buff thinks. *This is the best we can hope for?* Is he disappointed to find that the future is perfectly predict-able? Or is he relieved that it is still recognizable?

Is he supposed to see that the World of Tomorrow is no different from Luna Park's Trip to the Moon? A promise of a faraway land, an unforgettable voyage, an exotic leap of imagination that turns out to be … exactly what you had anticipated. Nothing more and nothing less. The highways are motorized; the moon-men are green.

The unknown is perfectly understandable; the future is familiar.

Or is it? he wonders.

Buff scratches his head and listens for music. He hears none.

Perhaps this world in the Perisphere is only a half truth.

And it is hiding the other half.

The one that sings louder.

The other half of the truth, Buff decides, is that the future cannot be seen. It is there, certainly, but like the dark side of the moon, it is hidden.

Buff leans further over the railing, and as he does, the pebble presses against his leg. He pulls it from his pocket and is not surprised to find it has turned pearly white. He holds it poised between thumb and forefinger above the World of Tomorrow… and lets go. It is tiny as it falls, but Buff thinks he can feel its energy magnified into a massive force.

Plink, says the pebble when it hits bottom – smooth

pavement with no place for loose pebbles. At the same moment, the megawatt lights clank off. The houses fill with smaller bulbs of kitchen light, the cars shine their headlights like fireflies, and the river twinkles in starlight. With that plink, daytime has ended in the World of Tomorrow and night has begun.

But something, thinks Buff, is missing.

He circles the raised gallery again, searching for night's missing note.

Light in the night. Dark in the day.

Lifting his gaze to the top of the great dome, he sees that there is no moon to light up the night in this World of Tomorrow. And Buff understands what lies inside the mermaid's pearl.

CHAPTER THIRTY-TWO

The Comfort Station, it turns out, is not a toilet for thirteen-year-old girls.

"You need to be with your guardian, young lady, and then we will be happy to demonstrate for you the latest advances in feminine apparel, including flexible rayon corsets, easy-snap-stays, ingenious boot insoles for the girl-on-the-go, and other remarkable innovations in female comfort."

"Oh for crying out loud," exclaims Paloma, "could ya just point me the way of the john? 'Cause I'm definitely a girl-on-the-go!"

The Comfort Station concierge does so, and Paloma joins the line for the ladies' room outside the domesticated livestock pavilion. It is a long line. She bounces on her toes. She hums a distracting tune. She shoves her hands in her pocket sand hops on one leg. Her tactics don't seem to be working and she breaks into a sweat.

"Ladies," she announces, when it seems the only solution, "we have a situation. I know it's impolite because yes, I do have a mother to tell me so – but if you ladies don't allow me to cut the line ..."

"Come on, then." A kind woman beckons from the front. But just as Paloma is about to reach the stall, another woman, mid-line, protests.

"I certainly don't see why my girls should be unfairly penalized for this young ragamuffin's impetuousness," she says tartly. Paloma turns to see a red-faced mother and her three pale daughters all looking down their noses at her. The daughters appear to be identical in every way except that one of them cannot be bothered to look bored, so instead she is grinning with buck teeth at Paloma's predicament.

"Good golly!" exclaims Paloma. "Is that how bad it gets in your family? Is that your idea of injustice? An unexpected holdup in the toity?"

There's an audible snicker from somewhere down the line. Paloma is just getting started. "Because if your little Polly or Molly or Dolly is about to have an embarrassing accident, well, heck – I can relate and I sure don't want to torment her any more. How 'bout it Molly? Think that bowl's big enough for the both of us?"

Now the snicker has turned to a gasp and the red-faced mother is calling for backup. "Security!" she hollers, grabbing Paloma by the elbow. But Paloma is off like a shot, worried less about the embarrassment of being arrested than of having wet trousers. She races down the nearest path, looking everywhere for another restroom, but there are only crowds, impeding her view and her ability to cover ground quickly. More and more desperate, Paloma jumps over the low chain that keeps pedestrians off the grass and makes a beeline for the privacy of foliage.

"You'd think I had escaped from the livestock barn," she giggles, squatting in the underbrush. Finished, she tidies herself up, buckles her overalls and begins to extricate herself from the bushes. She's in deeper than she realized, and when she emerges, she is not where she started. She is looking, not at the far-off Trylon and Perisphere, but at the weedy bank of Flushing Bay. And not two hundred feet away from her is Mingus Lamont, untying the mooring ropes of the Miasma.

When Buff feels the World of Tomorrow roll under his feet, he is neither frightened nor surprised. He understands that the source is far away and close to home. Something is moving in Coney Island. Something is shifting. Something, Buff understands, is hatching.

This realization – that the egg is ready and the time has come – sends him running down the ramp, out of the Perisphere, and across the Fairgrounds. He is racing the setting sun.

When he reaches the subway platform, Buff is short of breath. In a gasp he explains to Doc Couney that he needs to get back to Coney Island immediately. That there are children counting on him. That, more than that, all of Coney is counting on him. Well, not him. But on the egg.

The public address system crackles overhead. The Commissioner is being introduced by the Mayor as a man "of unparalleled vision of our nation's potential…"

"What is in the egg?" asks Doc Couney.

Vision, thinks Buff. Potential.

"The moon," he says. "The new moon."

Doc nods. He's a close watcher or the tides. He is as aware of the moon's phases as he is of a newborn's vitals.

"And how do you know?" he asks.

"Because it's the thing that is always there, hiding in plain sight. It's what is dark in the day and light in the night. It is what you see when you can't see at all. It's… hope."Buff's words are drowned by applause from the speakers. The cheers can be heard, unamplified, from the distant Trylon, and it is hard to distinguish which is the sound and which is the sound's shadow.

"Go to your egg," says Doc. "I vill vait for Paloma and follow you."

A quarter mile away, the Parks Commissioner mounts the steps of the Trylon Grandstand to address his grateful constituents. He taps the microphone and feels his heart thump in response to its amplified power. He grips the sides of the podium and feels his fingers relax in the familiar sensation of control.

"Good citizens of New York," he booms. "It is with great pride that I stand before you, here in the Heart of the Free World, to celebrate our Liberty and our Future."

Hiding behind a tree, Paloma curses the Commissioner and his blaring Public Address. It is Mingus Lamont she is trying to hear. The Steeplechase manager is standing at the end of a small dock, berating one of his Funny Face goons for sleeping on the job.

"Yeah, but I'm awake now, boss," protests Lou. "And it's not like I wanted to sleep. Heck no. I had to make myself sleep. If I'm gonna be watchman all night, last thing you want is a tired watchman. So I was just being, you know, smart. One step ahead of ya, boss."

"Watch your tongue, you punk, or you'll be one step ahead of me in the water. Now haul anchor. We gotta get back down to Steeplechase before the rest of you punks muck up the deal."

"I emptied out the hold just like you said. And I put extra rope in the boathouse so if any of 'em wake up on the ride, we can tie 'em up good."

"And you left some water in there too?"

"Yep. A barrel of water and all the week-old cookies."

"That's good. Wouldn't be much of a rescue if half of

the kids are dead of starvation when we rescue 'em."

"Pretty sure it takes more than a night to die of starvation, boss."

"Well – they're orphans, after all. No telling when the last time they et was."

"I knew it," Paloma whispers, and then, in her excitement, nearly shouts: "I knew it. I knew it was you, you toad! You sneaking, stealing, no-good thief!" Stepping out from behind the tree to accost the villains, Paloma runs smack into a fat man with a toothpick in his mouth. She turns to bolt, but the man trips her to the ground and places a thick-soled boot on her chest.

"I think maybe one of your midnight deliveries has arrived early, mister," he announces. A moment later, Paloma is looking up into the surprised faces of Mingus Lamont and Lou.

"This one. I know her." Lamont's voice is a blend of fear and ferocity. "And I'm inclined to think that she could have upended more than one apple barrel tonight."

Paloma sputters in indignation. "I'm on to you, Mingus Lamont! I'm not the only one who knows. Just the only one with proof, maybe. You won't get away with this, you thief! You smelly rat! You … kidnapper!"

253

"Hoist the girl up, Lou."

Now Lou has her by the waist and Lamont is walking back to the boat. He disappears into the cabin and Paloma gives Lou a kick in the shin. Lou's response is a smack to the back of her head, so that Paloma is already seeing stars when Lamont returns with a large glass jar under his arm.

"Even more important than cookies and milk," he is saying.

When he is so close that Paloma can smell the mildewed funk of his clothes, the Steeplechase manager unscrews the lid of the jar. She gets a whiff of something that overpowers Lamont's own stench.

"Smells like you peed your pants Ming…" she begins. But she is out cold before she finishes her taunt.

B uff stands close to the window of the subway train and watches the Trylon and Perisphere recede. *What could have happened to Paloma*, he worries. *Should I have waited?*

His concern builds, like a slow wave, into doubt: *Can I do this alone? Can I do this at all?*

But then Buff hears something that he alone can hear: a long low note and two short shots. In his mind's eye, he sees Handsome Henry standing on the beach, his lips in a whistle. Buff dives directly into his fear.

I can.

I will.

I will find them.

And Paloma Bright, wherever she is, will help light the way.

CHAPTER THIRTY-THREE

In the Steeplechase Warehouse Rita Chervinsky, aka Madame Fortuna, puts her foot down.

"Can't you see they don't want to play any more games, you dumb punks?"

"Sure they do. Mingus said so," says a short fellow with a long scar and several fresh scratches on his face.

"Where is Lamont?" she demands. "Why isn't he here?"

"I dunno. Maybe he's pickin' up the birthday cake," says the boy with the scar. From the shed comes a plaintive howl. "Caaaake! We want caaaake."

"See, now if you don't go do somethin' about that, they all of them are just gonna remember how the party was spoiled by there being no cake."

"I'm not doing it," Rita says again. "And what's more, I've already let Officer Ramsey know that two dozen kids should be reported missing if this birthday party don't end with all the kids back on the bus to Yonkers by nightfall." She looks at the place where the sun has set unseen. "And that was about twenty minutes ago."

The stare down between Madame Fortuna and scar-face doesn't last long. When the Steeplechase bully looks away, it is to pull a knife from his boot. His knife, Rita learns, is sharper than his gaze. She joins the children and their short-sighted guardian in the shack.

Mingus Lamont cranks the Miasma's motor to make up for lost time. He curses. The girl has delayed him. But not by much. Still, it's a bother that he had to leave his co-captain behind to make sure she doesn't cause more trouble. Not that she's likely too. She was full of so much hot air when he dunked her shnozz in the knock-out gas she'll likely sleep till Tuesday.

Now the Miasma is rounding the point. Just ten more minutes and he'll be docked at Steeplechase Pier. He squints into the distance, a crush of determined clouds.

Darker than it should be just an hour after sunset, he thinks.

The Wonder Wheel has just appeared in the window of the first car when the subway train stops in its tracks. Buff opens the window and looks out. They are stopped between stations. The streetlamps of Surf Avenue waver in the murk.

"Come on," he mutters, "come on."

But the train goes nowhere.

Cupping his hands around his eyes, Buff finds the moon in the sky. It is slimmer than a sliver. It is a collapsed crescent, a wink in the east, a fingernail moon, and it seems to be shrinking before his eyes. When it disappears, he will be ready.

When there is no moon to light the way – that is when your heart must shine.

Buff yanks open the carriage door and the tang of the sea bites the car.

The old lady huddled in the corner of the carriage is still scolding as the boy picks his way across the track and down the line to an escape ladder. He shimmies to the ground and for the second, but not the last, time that night, he runs as fast as he can.

The Mermother feels the heavy approach of the Miasma. She hears its tattered flag whip into life, startled by a strong gust of wind. That wind, she knows, is blowing the embers of resolve that smolder in Luna Park's heart. And that wind is pushing Buff south to Coney Island.

She can feel him draw near. The boy is on his way. He is bringing his newfound knowledge of the future – that it is uncertain and imperfect. He holds it in his hands, Coney Island's fresh start. He is bringing its new moon.

So what is it that sends a shiver through her waters?

The Miasma lets out a groan as it rubs along the Steeplechase Pier. Mingus Lamont kills the engine and throws a slimy rope to the masked boy standing ready.

"You want me to lower the anchor, boss?"

"Nah. We ain't gonna be here long enough for that."

Lamont squints into the gloom. In the sharp circle of light provided by the giant Funny Face he sees another of his goons leading a line of children along the boardwalk to the pier. The carny smiles. But his smile disappears when he sees that many of the twenty-four boys and girls are crying. Or kicking. Or whining.

He hurries forward and hisses, "Why the hell ain't these kids dopey?"

"Well, that soothsayin' lady," begins the guy with the scar. "She refused to say her sooth. She was acting pretty spooky so I left her locked her up in the shack with the dame from the orphanage."

Mingus Lamont throws his hat on the ground and stomps on it. He rages and jumps and rages some more. When he's done, a little boy at the head of the line says simply, "Hey, Mister. You were supposed to bring us cake."

Buff reaches the Incubator Baby House out of breath but full of energy. He hurries to the bassinet. The pearl is a pitch black ball of dark matter and stars shoot across its surface.

Breddy wants him to sit, she has so much to tell him, but Buff feels the press of time. He wraps the egg in a baby blanket and tucks it into his rucksack. He is halfway out the door when he reconsiders. He turns back to the nurse who has mothered him all his life and puts his arms around her.

"What is it you wanted to tell me?"

"There are more children missing."

"I know. But they're coming back."

Breddy shakes her head. She doesn't believe its possible, but then, it's been a night full of the unbelievable.

Henry and Myrtle make their stealthy way towards Steeplechase Park. Myrtle leads. She is more familiar with the route they have chosen – the path underneath the boardwalk. Henry is dressed from head to toe in the black rubber of the frog-man's suit. His mustache is freshly waxed. Myrtle carries an electrician's kit. Her wild hair is tied up in a scarf. They stop, just underneath the Pavilion of Fun, and exchange a few words.

"This is my stop. But the path goes all the way to the canal. Clyde'll meet you there."

"Be careful."

"Not really my strong point, Handsome."

"Then be reckless."

"Now yer talkin'."

And there in the high arches of the wooden hinge between boardwalk and pier, the bally-man and the mermaid queen exchange their first kiss.

Out on Coney Island Creek, Clyde is crowing with delight. The Mickey is waterborne. A bit sputtery, and the steering wheel takes some adjusting for, since the old boat wants to list leeward, but the Mick's kicked up to eleven knots and hasn't stalled once.

"Won't that bally-man be pleased when we come burstin' outta the canal?" shouts the Captain as he leans into the spray of the Mickey's forward thrust, his eyes on the narrow weir that separates the western end of the creek from the bay. "Now ready them sucker cups, matey, we have a rogue vessel to lasso."

Behind him, Greta Gershwin sits impassively. In one hand, she brandishes a nail gun. In the other, she cradles a giant octopus.

"Aye aye, Captain," she says.

The Steeplechase manager is still staring at the kid who wants cake. The giant electric Funny Face is reflected in the boy's bright eyes, and it is laughing at him. Yes. Laughing. It's as if someone has pulled a mask off and for the first time, Mingus Lamont sees clearly. He sees... a bad situation. Bad. Bad. Bad. Because it is not just that loud-mouthed girl Paloma who knows what he has done. That, he could handle. And the busy-body from Yonkers who brought all the brats. And maybe even Rita too. But it's not just them. It's these twenty-four nasty little cake-eaters. How was he going to keep them yapping now that they have stood here on his pier, seen him stomp on his hat, and smelled the bowels of the Miasma?

Desperate times, he decides, call for desperate measures.

Lamont summons Jinx and Bugs to his side and lowers his voice as he dispatches Jinx to the warehouse for enough chain link to wrap around twenty-four skinny legs. Then the craft carny turns to Bugs. "And I want you to get a wheelbarrow and fill it with bowling balls from the bowling alley. The heaviest ones. A drill too."

Bugs, who is not as dumb as he looks, looks from his boss to the waiting kids to the Miasma and back to his boss.

"Ming…" he says.

"Do it and you won't go down with them," hisses Lamont.

Buff steps out into the night and inhales. He smells the familiar funk but also, a ripple within it, a fresh scent. It smells urgent, it smells latent. It smells like something about to burst into flame. He closes his eyes and breathes slowly.

He's listening for a song, a melody, a whistle. For a long minute, there is nothing. He opens his eyes and looks up. Heavy clouds bump across the sky, smothering the tiny bright crack of the moon. Out of the corner of his eye Buff sees the top gondola of the Wonder Wheel swing wildly in the wind.

Light in the night, he thinks.

A beacon.

A message.

He crosses Surf Avenue and squeezes through the gate of the darkened Ferris wheel. He makes his way to the operator's booth, where he pulls a flashlight from his bag and begins searching the mechanical panels. A row of switches controls the electric bulbs that spell:

W-O-N-D-E-R

W-H-E-E-L

across the wheel's great spokes. Buff flips two of them. Then he flips two more. He hurries back out of the booth and runs the short distance to the boardwalk to survey his work. It is a message that beams dimly but defiantly against the dark; it is a message of solidarity.

W   E...blazes the six-foot rallying cry,

W E

And the night answers back:

LOOKA! from Coney Island Creek.

LOOKA! from the Sideshow.

LOOKA! from under the boardwalk.

Buff grins. They are all in place. From all corners, Coney's carnies have rallied in solidarity.

W E...come to help.

W E...the Ring around Luna.

Buff hitches the straps of his rucksack tighter, feels the egg leap inside, and starts running again.

*T*he Mermother swims to the surface. The sky is black. Clouds gather in the dark like guerilla fighters. Coney Island is crackling with messages and her skin soaks them up, runs them along her scales, decodes them easily.

LOOKA, LOOKA, LOOKA ...

The taunt of Steeplechase has been thrown back in its Funny Face. The message from the Wonder Wheel is all that's important now. The men and women of Coney Island have woken from a stupor. They are ready to make their own fireworks.

You've done it, Buff, she thinks. You've drawn the lines, you've summoned the troops, now all you must do is let loose the new moon…and they will all come home.

She is just about to dive back under the waves, when an unhappy shout from the west stops her. She turns and sees a small puddle of light splashed on the Steeplechase Pier. The Mermother holds perfectly still, straining her limpid green eyes to see. And when she does, she gasps. Because a procession of two dozen children, linked at the ankles with chains, is shuffling into that pool of light.

Oh, Buff. I can't wait any longer.

CHAPTER THIRTY-FOUR

Doc Couney is losing his patience in the police head-quarters next to the Telephony Theater. The cops in their spiffy uniforms watch him warily. They are not happy about his information: a girl has gone missing at the World's Fair.

"That doesn't happen here," is what the desk officer said when the doctor first approached him. When the old man insisted that indeed it had, the policeman asked him to lower his voice and take a seat.

"We will initiate protocol," he told the doctor. What he didn't tell him was that "protocol," when it comes to anything suggesting bad news for the Fair, consists of reporting directly to the Commissioner, who would then determine whether the event was an "Incident" or a "Non-Incident." He also did not tell the worried doctor that lost children are under no circumstances to be treated as an "Incident," until personally investigated by the Commissioner.

And so Doc waits, listening, along with the police officer and everyone within five miles of the Trylon, to the strident voice of the Commissioner proclaiming over the

PA system a "New Day for New York and for the World."

When the speech is finally over, Doc approaches the desk officer. "I vould like you to tell me vat you aim to do about my ..."

He is interrupted. The Commissioner is already in the room and he is yelling.

"Who took the report of a missing ..." His eyes land on Doc Couney.

"I dunno who took it, but I'm the one dat brung it and now I vould like you to do somesink about it," answers the doctor. "The young girl whom to you I introduced earlier, she is gone for more dan one hour. But not one of your officers seem inclined to help me find her. Now if dis was Coney Island, I might understand. Our local officials have been known to get kleine defeated what mit ze cutbacks and hardships and lack of ze manpower. But I don't sink zese conditions apply here on your, shall we say, turf, Mr. Commissioner."

As Doc speaks, the Commissioner feels anxiety creep back to visit him and leave a knot in his chest. "What about the boy?" he asks, surprised that his voice is a whisper.

"Buff? He's gone home. He had ... vell, he's gone home."

The Commissioner exhales. "Well then, the girl has probably joined him. Kids are impulsive like that. I propose we notify the Coney Island precinct," he says.

He calmly picks up the phone and places the call, which

is answered after several rings by Officer Sherman Ramsey. Ramsey interrupts the Commissioner's brusque instructions to inform him that he has no men to dispatch or be on the lookout for anything other than the twenty-four confirmed missing persons in Coney Island tonight. "You hear that, Mr. Commissioner? Twenty-four kids gone missing! And if you'll pardon me for sayin' so – you gotta helluva lotta nerve, sir. A helluva lotta nerve."

And with that, the call is dropped.

The Commissioner stares blankly at the receiver. "Twenty-four children," he mumbles. The knot is his chest tightens, as before him the weasel face of Mingus Lamont swims and stammers.

Two dozen specimens. Delivery set …

The Commissioner struggles to remember what he had said to the Steeplechase manager in response to this cryptic message.

Did I approve this plan? he wonders.

Of course not.

But did I reject it?

His palms moist and his brow furrowed, he gazes out the window at his pristine World of Tomorrow. On your turf, the doctor had said. The Commissioner thinks of the lush green turf from Steeplechase that now carpets the south lawn. He thinks of the checks on the accounting books made out to Mingus Lamont. He senses disaster.

For a moment, time freezes as the unhappy Commissioner imagines worst-possible scenarios: the City's most trusted guardian implicated in a dastardly kidnapping plot; every victory he has scored for the People, forfeited because of a single Missing Person ; the headlines dragging him from honor, from power, from history. It is breathtakingly awful.

"Steno!" he barks, "I want an APB on the missing girl NOW and I want a sketch. Dr. Couney here will assist you in the description."

He grabs the desk officer by the collar and draws him close to deliver private instructions: "When she's found I want her secured, far from the press," he says in a low voice. "Don't let her speak to anyone until I return."

He nods at the old man. "Not even him."

The officer salutes smartly and picks up his radio transmitter.

"Get my car," the Commissioner orders next.

He turns back to the doctor, who is watching the police scurry into action.

"I will fix this, I assure you," says the New York City Parks Commissioner, reaching for his hat. "I will fix this before …"

He doesn't finish his thought, but as he sweeps out of the police headquarters he thinks, *before I am ruined.*

CHAPTER THIRTY-FIVE

Paloma wakes in the dark with a pounding headache. It pounds so hard and aches so bad that she doesn't immediately notice the dark. In fact, it takes some time before she realizes that her eyes are open, her head is in one piece, and her hands and feet are bound.

"Sweet Shirley Temple," she thinks. "Those bastards have me roped up."

Her next thought is that her head hurts. After that, that those bullfrogs are making an ungodly racket and then, that the ropes around her wrists would probably cut like butter if she could just find something to cut them with.

And that when it hits her. The dark.

In an instant, Paloma's predicament turns to panic. She is alone in the dark. And it's not the dark of home, which she knows how to dilute with fireflies and candles and glow in the dark gizmos. It's the dark of being stolen. She holds her breath and hears her heart beating in fear, drowning out the bullfrogs. Paloma waits five long seconds and then bursts into frightened tears. She only stops when a muffled boom echoes outside her prison and a flash of light finds its way through a crack behind her. Scrambling awkwardly over the splintered floor, she presses her face to the crack and sees the light cascade of sparks.

The fireworks have begun over the Fairground, and the kidnapped girl takes heart.

Brushing away her tears with bound hands, Paloma Bright concentrates on the light – the light in the night. She imagines the glow of her kitchen window above Bettleman's Dancehall; the fire-spark breath of Angelica DeMicco and the flame-red hair of Myrtle Crespi; she thinks of the luminous glow of the mysterious egg and the light that her friend Buff always sees at the end of the tunnel.

There are clues in the World of Tomorrow, he had said. There is hope.

Paloma clenches her fists and sings the song she heard him sing so long ago – back when she thought that she was the safe one:

Ring around the Luna,
Pocket full of tuna,
Ashes, ashes,
We all come home.

"I'm coming home!" she announces to the dark. In the light of the next flash of fireworks, Paloma finds a loose nail in the floorboards and uses it to sever the rope around her wrists. Still singing, she unties her feet and then, using the same nail, picks the lock on the boathouse door. She kicks it open and springs out into the night.

Immediately and simultaneously, three things become clear. The first is that a crazy wild wind is shaking all the trees of Flushing Bay. The second is that Lou, sprawled in an old lawn chair on the dock, has seen her escape. But the last and most alarming thing that dawns on Paloma in the instant of her own freedom is this – the meaning of the Miasma schedule's code:

742dozbrats2030high: July 4, 7-4. 2030, 8:30.

In a matter of hours, two dozen children will be spirited away on a high tide.

She has to stop the Miasma.

Her pounding head forgotten, Paloma Bright takes off running, and Lou takes off after her.

There are pyrotechnics at Coney Island, too. They come from the Steeplechase Pavilion of Fun. Myrtle Crespi has climbed onto the roof and is having some fun with the Funny Face's circuit board.

Mingus Lamont is still giving orders ("Find that boy, the story-teller from Luna Park and bring him here!") when he notices it: The Funny Face is going haywire. There is a flash and a loud crack, and then another and another, as every light bulb of the oversize grin takes part in an explosion of tungsten.

"What the ..." mutters Lamont as a thread of blue fire wiggles its way across the great glass windows and shoots through the broken panes. But he has no time to investigate. Another exclamation from his crew is more urgent: "What the!?"

Mingus Lamont turns his back on the Funny Face and stares in disbelief. There is a long chain of shackled bowling balls lying in front of the cargo hold of the Miasma. Moments ago, each of those bowling balls had been attached to a pair of unfortunate feet. But now the pier is empty, except for his confused goons.

"They just ... went ... poof," explains Bugs, unhelpfully. He has removed his mask, to better search the dark water for his vanished captives, who perhaps have slipped their shackles and shimmied down the pylons. "The kids just ... went ... poof."

A hundred yards east, a flash of gilt green breaks the water and then submerges into a pool of bubbles. It's a sight unseen by Mingus and gang on the pier, but on the roof of the Steeplechase Pavilion, Myrtle Crespi puts down her wire cutters and rips the safety goggles from her face to get a better look at what she could swear was ... a mermaid.

Buff smells smoke. Something is burning. Emerging from Wonder Walk he sees it - the Pavilion of Fun is on fire. The flames are rushing towards the wooden Thunderbolt. Buff thinks of the warehouse below the roller coaster – and of the shack meant as a waiting room for two dozen kidnapped children.

His rucksack is heavy and urgent, but he knows the children must come first. He needs to know if Henry has caught the kid-catcher.

"They're all in the water," says a voice at his side.

Buff jumps, startled by Angelica DeMicco's camouflaged face. With her torches strapped in a harness and her flask tucked in her belt, the Flame Eating Totem is a human ignition and a tattooed bounty hunter.

"Who's in the water?"

"Everybody. Henry, Clyde, Greta. Myrtle's taking care of the Funny Face. Everyone is in place…"

"But the children – where are the children?"

Buff is studying the flame-eater, confused by the inky profile painted across her wide cheeks. It's as if she is looking in both directions—east towards Dreamland Pier and west towards Steeplechase Pier—and at the same time, she is looking out to sea.

He's about to ask again if Henry has rescued the children, when he hears the sound of hobnailed boots pounding down the stairs from the boardwalk.

"That's him! That's the one! Get him!"

Angelica grabs Buff's arm and they run. Down the walk and into the warren of amusements. The flame-eater darts right, and Buff follows her into a narrow alley lined with games of chance. At the top of the alley, Angelica skids to a stop and hollers, "High noon!" A dozen metal roll-up gates rattle open on either side and a hundred water-gun pistols take aim. "Watch this," says Angelica as their pursuers are caught in a well-planned, watery ambush.

But there are more Funny Faces on the hunt. They are waiting in the shadows of the Dodge 'em Cars. Buff spies them and looks to the flame-eater for a signal. She gives him a nod and he climbs the fence onto the speedway. Three masked boys clamor towards him, but he stands fast as Angelica pushes the start button on each and every car. By the time Buff reaches the far side, he has only one pursuer left – a shoeless one, his boot now a hood ornament on a demonic driverless car.

Now the Steeplechase gate is in sight.

Ashes, ashes … warns the voice in Buff's head. The Pavilion is coming apart, scattering flaming debris into the lot where the warehouse hunkers. Buff slides under the fence, crosses the lot and pushes into the warehouse. He scrambles through the debris and smoke and finds the skimpy shed. It's locked.

"Hang on!" he shouts. "I'll get you out!"

Grabbing an old track hammer with strength he didn't think he had, Buff batters down the door. Inside is a bedraggled woman he has never seen. She is coughing uncontrollably and her shortsighted eyes are red from smoke. Next to her sits Madame Fortuna, calmly laying out her deck of Tarot cards. She removes the scarf she has wrapped around her mouth and nose and says, "Well. It's about time."

CHAPTER THIRTY-SIX

Paloma pauses in the bright white glow of the main Fairgrounds. The fireworks have reached their climax, and everywhere she looks are the shining upturned faces of a marveling crowd. Paloma feels a strange dislocation. An uneasy calm. Her gaze grows glassy in the floodlit Future, and for a moment she forgets her urgency. She sways slightly, mesmerized by the artificial lights and stunned by the bold symmetry of the Trylon and Perisphere. The crowd ooohs and the crowd ahhs and the wind picks up, but Paloma is somewhere else. She feels a million miles from home. She feels she could be on the moon. The spell is broken by the squawk of a radio. A policeman is standing ten feet away. Like all the cops in the World of Tomorrow, he sports a state-of-the-art communication device. A portable two-way radio.

"Sector Five – any sign of the girl?" asks the radio.

Paloma thrills, remembering. They are looking for her!

The radio crackles again: "Attention all sectors. Subject is to be held. Repeat. When found, subject to be detained until Commissioner's orders."

Paloma despairs. They are looking for her. But "they" are the Commissioner's police. She remembers the steely grip on her shoulder. She remembers his impatient face and all it revealed – the Commissioner cares more about getting an Incubator House for his Fair than he does about the babies inside it. She can't trust him any more than that toady, Mingus Lamont. She is on her own. On her own and far from home.

The cop pulls out his radio and confirms the orders to detain the girl by any means. As he is returning it to his belt he does a double-take. He has seen her.

And he's not the only one. There's a shout from behind, from the woods. Lou has caught up.

Paloma runs again.

A stern black car pulls to a halt on Stillwell Avenue. The Commissioner unfolds his long frame from the back and without a single glance at the burning Pavilion next to him, climbs the stairs to the boardwalk pier, where he grabs Mingus Lamont by the scruff of the neck.

"You are a disgrace," he says quietly to the man whose feet dangle helplessly in the air. "I want you to know that I will denounce you. I will deny you. And if anything has happened to the girl...I will destroy you."

Lamont snivels and claws at the big hand encircling his throat. But he can't speak.

"Now what other heinous cargo have you stowed on that miserable ship of yours? Where are those children?"

Lamont gestures desperately at his throat and gasps something about "inventory changes."

The Commissioner loosens his grip to let the man talk.

"We had them," hacks Mingus. "But they got away. We were gonna take 'em to the Fair just like you said but that no-good Rita …"

The Commissioner twists Lamont's collar back into a noose.

"Where. Are. The. Children."

"I dunno, your honor. They ain't here. We … we let 'em go," squeaks Lamont.

The Commissioner drops the little man into a heap. Then he pulls a handkerchief from his pocket, wipes his hands fastidiously, and strides down the pier towards the hulking boat. At its ladder he turns back to Mingus Lamont and the humiliated remnants of his gang. "All hands on deck!" he barks. Then he boards the boat as if he were born at sea.

A moment later, the Miasma sends a bilious fart into the water and pulls away from the pier. As it does, a second boat, smaller and significantly less sturdy, emerges from the concrete weir further down the beach and points its bow towards the Miasma's wake.

Steeplechase is burning. Buff says, "We have to go." But Madame Fortuna is calmly turning out her cards. "Someone's plans have been laid low." She lays a finger on a card that shows a tall tower struck by lightening. Its windows are in flames and its peaked roof is plummeting to the earth. So, too, are its inhabitants – a king and his page, their faces masked in fear.

She flips another card from her deck and places it crosswise over the tower. It shows a woman with golden hair, a crown of stars and a gown pleated with seahorses.

"The Empress gives life. From the sea and from the moon. She is a water sign and she allies with the sun sign."

The fortune-teller glances up at Buff and studies him closely. Then she turns a third card and nods in recognition. "An innocent, trusting his heart," she says softly to the picture of a wanderer carrying a rucksack not unlike Buff's.

The boy flushes. "Rita – there's no time. We have to go."

"Never seen that," she says, studying the next card with its picture of an upside down nest. "A mother that's a boy-child?" she guesses. "A birth from a watery bed?"

"We have to get to the beach," says Buff. "Please."

They step out of the shed, the wobbly woman from Yonkers between them. Outside the air is thick with smoke. From its black depths emerges one last determined Funny Face. It's Snake, and he holds a flaming torch.

"Move it, sonny," growls Rita. "You've got no dog left in this fight."

But Snake is undeterred. He pushes the women and the boy backwards against the warehouse and pulls metal cuffs from his belt. He is just about to clamp them on Buff when his torch explodes in a fireball. Yelling in terror, Snake rips the flaming mask from his face and races for the boating pond, his hair ablaze.

Angelica DeMicco steps out of the wavering heat, her lips glistening with kerosene. She wipes her mouth with the back of her hand, tucks her flask back into her belt, and spits. She lifts her tattooed silhouette above the smoky pall and Buff follows her gaze. There, high above the Narrows, he sees another silhouette. It is the frame of the moon, hiding in its own darkness. It is a pocket for the new moon.

"Pocket for the luna," he says.

"Ashes, ashes," replies the flame-eater.

Buff doesn't wait to hear the last line. He hurries to catch the children — before they all fall down.

CHAPTER THIRTY-SEVEN

Paloma runs until she finds herself alone. Nearly alone. The fireworks have drawn the bulk of the crowd to the Trylon. Here, in a lonely no-man's land, she catches her breath. But she knows her pursuers are close behind.

She bends, hands on knees, and listens to the distant squawk of radios.

Headed towards the Midway. In pursuit.

Paloma jolts upright and scans her horizons. Sure enough, behind her and over a low ridge she can see the lights of the Midway, the area designated to amusements and rides. She hears the sound of a calliope and the chug of a kids' coaster on tracks, and she runs for their familiar embrace.

Once inside the lively gates of the Midway, she ducks behind a dumpster to avoid another handful of cops fanning out at the entrance. When the coast is clear, she creeps out and joins a large group wandering aimlessly until they reach an open square flanked with souvenir stands and balloon twisters.

In the center of the square is the wide metal base of

a tower. Craning her neck, Paloma follows the lattice of struts upwards to the top of the tower–a broad hat like a steel sombrero. She feels a flash of recognition. It's the Parachute Jump that Ramsey had described. But she knows it better as her secret joke with Buff ...

"The Interborough Super Suck."

A wide grin crosses her face as a wild wind crosses the square, whipping skirts, hats and popcorn bags as it passes. Paloma's mind is racing as she studies the unique structure.

What if? she thinks as she watches the circle of swings rise slowly until only the soles of the feet of the Parachute Jumpers are visible.

Why not? she asks as she prays for a magical portal between Flushing Bay and Coney Island.

The swings pause at the top, rocking in anticipation. Paloma holds her breath as another gust of wind elicits a shriek from one of the riders. Then with a whir and a jolt and another shriek, all twelve swings drop at once. Seconds later, the parachutes snap open like the petals of a flower in bloom, and the riders float serenely to the ground. Safely back on land, the jumpers are released from the swings. They hop off and run, laughing, through another buffet of wind.

Paloma stands at the base of the Parachute Jump, watching and thinking. She smells seasalt. She spies a lone balloon catapulting head over heels on an airborne current. She has a crazy idea.

In a heartbeat the girl from Coney Island is at the front of the line. In another, she is strapped onto one of the swings. She is already fifteen feet off the ground when she sees Lou bulldoze his way through the square to the base of the Jump.

"Faster," she mutters, turning her face upward. "Faster."

When the top comes into view, Paloma can see the system of straps and cables that harness her to the swing and the swing to the tower. Her eyes dart across the gear, puzzling out its mechanism. The wind whistles through the lattice work of the upper ring and a friendly face appears next to her. The Jump jockey holds out his hand to steady her unopened chute.

"Wind's pickin up!" he yells. "Last ride of the night!"

"Say! Which of these belts keeps me from flying out to sea?" Paloma asks innocently. The Jump jockey grins. "All of them!" he says. Then he taps a large leather hook and latch just above Paloma's head. "But this one here is the key."

Paloma's stomach is doing flips and flops as she looks down at the ground. There is tiny Lou waving a tiny brass-knuckled fist. Surrounding him is a swarm of tiny policemen. Further out on the Great White Way, a caravan of tiny squad cars are descending on the Midway.

"Catch me if you can," she whispers.

Then she turns to the Jump jockey and yells above the howling wind: "I want you to know that I take full responsibility for this! And I sure hope it's a good show!"

The ride operator grabs his ears and shakes his head with another grin to indicate he can't hear what she's saying.

"We all fall down!" she hollers, and he nods, still deaf to her message. Then she reaches up, presses the latch of the heavy cable hook and falls. The Jump jockey shouts, the crowd on the ground swoons, and the police radios go berserk.

But Paloma hears none of it.

She doesn't even hear her own scream as, a hundred feet from the ground, she is snatched from the jaws of Lou, the police and the asphalt of the Great White Way by the snap of the parachute as it catches a gale force above Flushing Bay and propels her, a small bird in mid-summer flight, south towards Coney Island.

Chapter Thirty-Eight

Once Steeplechase Pier has vanished in smoke, The Commissioner leaves the helm. Out on the deck he pulls the trapdoor open and lowers himself into the Miasma's hold. Its emptiness confirms that there is no one to save and nothing to gain by turning the ship over to the so-called authorities.

He returns to the cabin, where he seizes the ship's logs and rips the pages from its spine with one hand. He snatches a burning cigarette from one of the sullen Funny Faces and holds it to the pages. The records smolder, but the Commissioner is impatient. He drops them half-burnt into the ocean.

Now the eagle eyes of the man who sees nothing good on Brooklyn's southern shore scan the Coney Island skyline and spot easy pickings. Steeplechase is in flames, the boardwalk is bereft. The bungalows left and right – they are already nearly invisible in the smoky haze. The Commissioner turns his back on the mainland and faces the open water. Another quarter of a mile, he calculates, and his reputation will be secure. He will open the cargo bay and sink the Miasma. Only then can he be safe – when the proof that the New York City Parks Commissioner had once made a deal with a devil is lying on the bottom of the sea.

Clyde has cut the Mickey's motor to avoid detection, but Handsome Henry is just as impatient as the Commissioner. He clambered aboard the Mick before the Miasma left the pier, and he has been imagining the hold full of frightened children ever since.

"I'm going in," he says when they are about two hundred feet away from the bigger boat. He stands and accepts the tools offered by Clyde's melancholic first-mate. Greta pumps the cylinder of the nail gun. "Make a neat perforation and let my pet, here, do the rest," she says, stroking the blood red creature in her lap. "He takes some prodding. But when he finds his mark, he won't let go... ever."

Henry considers this. "Ever?"

"Ever."

"So I shouldn't worry about returning him?"

"I have others."

Greta bends her spooky head and kisses the small octopus on what is likely its head. Then she hands it to the bally-man, who wrestles it under one arm.

"Godspeed, boyo," says Clyde as Henry swings his

legs over the side of the Mickey and adjusts his goggles. "We'll sidle up quiet while you do your thing."

Henry takes a swift look at the burning Pavilion of Fun. Then he nods and drops into the dark water with his extra-handy companion.

The first of the fire trucks has arrived on Surf Avenue. There to meet them is Myrtle Crespi, her face blackened and her eyes on fire."Aim all your hoses at Steeplechase, boys," she says. "But we'll be needing any extra nets you can lend. Got a whole school of guppies to catch, and a nasty bottom feeder too."

The Commissioner and Mingus Lamont are sweating in the Miasma's close cabin and hating each other equally.

"Everything woulda worked out swell," whines Mingus, "if it weren't for that treacherous Rita Chervinsky. Low-life, double crosser, she is. And obviously, what with no insurance that the kids wouldn't blab, well, I had no choice but to abort. Yeah. That's it. Gotta stay flexible if you're a man of action, like you and me."

The Commissioner looks at the sniveling carny and arches an eyebrow. He opens the cabin door and gestures for the carny to look: The last of the Funny Faces is diving overboard and striking out for shore.

"Observe, Mr. Lamont. Your deck is empty. Your crew has deserted you. And your park …is on fire."

Mingus peeks out the cabin door and yelps sadly.

"Furthermore, your reckless actions are incontrovertible evidence of this wretched den's depravity. You are a resounding success. I couldn't have wrecked Coney Island better myself," concludes the Commissioner.

For a moment, Mingus Lamont perks up. But then the Commissioner shoves him into a closet of buckets. At the helm, the Commissioner grasps a lever and pulls it, ignoring the flashing red light and throbbing siren that indicates that the cargo hull is open … when it should not be.

"No, indeed," he says as he crosses back to the deck and climbs into the only lifeboat on board. "Even if I were an evil little kidnapper like you, Mr. Lamont, I could not have wrecked Coney Island better myself."

Water is already pouring into the Miasma's underside as the Commissioner lowers himself over the side of the boat and positions his getaway east towards the Rockaways. "But I will, Mr. Lamont," he says between clenched teeth. "I will wreck it better."

Lamont scurries to the starboard side and watches his former patron square his broad shoulders and pull hard on the oars. A rat afraid to jump ship, Mingus Lamont is alone on the Miasma.

Alone, that is, except for Handsome Henry and his

now-unnecessarily strong-suckered companion. The bally man's chest is nearly bursting as he peers into the waterlogged depths of the ship's empty hold and wonders how he has come to fail once again.

Buff finds Officer Ramsey on the Steeplechase Pier looking blindly out to sea. Visibility is poor. Visibility is null. Somewhere out there the Miasma is sinking, the Commissioner is escaping, and Henry is despairing. But Coney Island is still in the dark.

Ramsey - no World's Fair cop - has to make do with a giant bullhorn to communicate with Clyde. It's rough going, given the wind, the waves and Clyde's thick Irish brogue.

"Aye, we got us a slippery catch, we do!" comes Clyde's voice from somewhere near but not near enough to see. "Churnin' up the water like I ain't seen since the mackerel run of '23."

"Twenty-three?" repeats Ramsey as he consults with the lady from Yonkers who is wringing her hands with worry. "Clyde, gimme a headcount! Are all the children accounted for? And what's happening with the ship? Over." Firefighters rush past the policeman, ready to cast their nets for the children.

"Went down, she did," booms Clyde. There's another long silence. When next they hear Clyde's voice, it is much closer.

"Sure. Hope you have room in the precinct house ..." it says. "I wouldn't let none of 'em ... pipe down ya briny ... in the Mick..."

The Mickey appears suddenly in the smoky dark. Captained by Clyde, manned by Henry and Greta, and trailing a heavily laden fishing-net, the little boat docks at the pier. Buff and Ramsey hurry forward. The net, they see, is dragging Mingus Lamont and his sodden Funny Faces.

Myrtle Crespi comes flying down the pier. "Where are they?" she asks, looking in vain for the kidnapped children.

Henry is the first out of the boat. Buff has never seen his eyes so dead, his mustache so indifferent, his body so limp.

"It was empty," he says simply. "Empty as a pocket."

Buff raises his head and looks once more for the empty pocket in the sky. It is visible, for just a moment – a black shadow hidden in a blacker night, the moon's perimeter. And then it is covered by the cloak of clouds.

He looks back at his friends, distracted by the immediacy of their concerns: Myrtle holds the wet Henry in her arms; Ramsey and Clyde are hauling the bad guys on deck; Lionel Bangs has lugged a hose all the way from Luna Park and joined the firemen at the burning pavilion; Rita Chervinsky and Angelica are bandaging the head of a singed Snake.

Buff kicks off his shoes and jumps to the beach. He runs east to the Dreamland Pier. A minute later, Coney Island's scrawniest citizen, a motherless runt, is swimming through high tide with a magical egg strapped to his back.

Only Madame Fortuna sees him go.

An innocent trusting his heart, she thinks. But she keeps her big mouth shut.

CHAPTER THIRTY-NINE

If it weren't for the dragonfly, Paloma's mouth would have stayed open all the way from Flushing to Brooklyn. *Phwaat*, she splutters. She's already forgotten the bug, just as she has forgotten the pins and needles in her feet. Just as she has forgotten the nagging question about what she should do when it comes time to land at the end of the line – Coney Island, next stop, the Atlantic Ocean.

Because at the moment, Paloma Bright is sailing southward with a swift wind at her back. And she's having the time of her life. Compared to this (she will think some time later), the Thunderbolt is a rocking horse; the Wonder Wheel, a hamster's toy; the Perisphere, a dullard's model of a tepid world.

Not long ago she passed over the World's Fair in all its glory. She marveled at its geometric precision. But it was the sight of Doc Couney pointing up, pointing at Paloma, smacking his head and breaking into a jig, that most delighted her.

"Come on, old man!" she hollered. "Get those cops down to Coney pronto!"

Whether he heard her or not, Doc Couney followed orders. She saw him run to the nearest squad car, point once more, and climb quickly into the back seat. In no time, a convoy of flashing blue lights was headed south with Paloma.

The wind whistles in her ears and Paloma squints into the night. The city passing underneath her is quiet and strung with streetlights. She follows the strands until her eyes dance cloverleaf patterns. She turns her head to be sure that she still has her police escort. Sure enough, there is Doc, standing in an open car like he's the hero of a ticker-tape parade. She waves and he lifts his fist in answer.

"Go on, Doc!" she cries. "Time's a-wastin'!"

A flight of seagulls careens into her path and then splits to flank her.

"Go on," she says again, to herself now. "I got a new escort. And they have wings."

As if in answer, the sirens wail and the cars race ahead towards Coney Island.

The wind roars anew, nearly tumbling Paloma from her swing, and the heavy cloudbank before her splits like a highway of light through the dark night.

Buff clambers onto the buoy, his hair dripping and his rucksack sodden. The surf is whipped up with strange winds and the sucking weight of a sinking ship.

Buff braces against the waves, crouching for balance. For a moment he feels victorious: I made it to the buoy. So the children must be safe. He imagines hundreds of baby sea-turtles cheering. Then he pictures the untouched whiteness of one dead turtle, belly-up in the moonlight.

Still squatting, he pulls the egg from his waterlogged bag and places it gently on the rusty plate of the barnacled bell.

It is a planet full of fissures. Its dark surface teems with tiny threads of light. The platform stills.

Shine bright in the darkness, the boy whispers to the egg as it flashes with its own fireworks. Then Buff rings the bell and the egg … hatches.

The parachute is chopping through lower Brooklyn like a drunken homing pigeon and Paloma pulls valiantly at cords as she cruises over rooftops with inches to spare. She smells the tang of the sea and the tickle of smoke. Scrambling to her knees, Paloma gasps at the sight of Coney Island on fire. Scanning the boardwalk, she sees that it is Steeplechase burning and that fire engines are already parked in a confused cluster with the police trucks from Flushing.

She yanks at her harness and banks left with the gulls. She's setting a course for the Wonder Wheel which is spinning like a fan, blowing smoke out to sea. Now the minarets and cupolas of Luna Park are visible, emerging modestly in their no-longer-brilliant coats of white paint.

And then Paloma spots something new in the familiar park: there, surrounded by the bamboo stand just behind the park's main gate is the abandoned dark ride, The Trip to the Moon. From on high, it is clearly visible, and not just because Paloma has a bird's eye view – The Trip to the Moon is circled by a fuzzy blue halo.

"Ring around the Luna," whispers Paloma.

And then the sky over Coney Island explodes.

Afterwards, everyone who saw it will have trouble agreeing on what it was. The carnies on the pier, the Steeplechase rats, the cops, the firefighters and every kid from Brighton to Norton's Point who saw the fireworks from their window – all of them will remember something different, but with the same vividness. Where one saw the Cyclone running six trains at once, another saw skyscrapers built on its tracks. Where one saw a bridge soaring over the Narrows, another saw a barge carrying windowless towers.

Clyde sees a typhoon forming;

Ramsey sees a medal with stars, and Doc sees an alpine meadow full of celestial flowers.

From his selfish dinghy far out to sea, the Commissioner sees the time-lapse arc of a wrecking ball.

Buff sees the egg crack and spill an ethereal moonlight down the sides of the floating platform and sink in rivulets into the ocean. He sees a bolt of light launch from its shattered surface and pierce the heavy blanket above. He covers his eyes to protect them from the blinding radiance, but when he looks again he sees the clouds in retreat, revealing an electric sky filled with megawatt minnows and shooting stars.

On the beach, Henry drops his eyes from the fantastical sky to the distant buoy ... and sees his brave young friend slide senseless into the water.

This time, Henry arrives on time.

Paloma jerks her head up and sees stars, stripes, bells and whistles. She sees raised fists and open mouths and tears of joy track across the sky. She whoops and breaks into applause. Then she sees the silk of the parachute as it slumps across her face and clutches the ropes.

"Incoming!" she shouts as the boardwalk rises to meet her.

Buff and Henry stagger up the beach. The boy is holding the bally-man's hand and squeezing it tight.

"Don't worry, Handsome," he says. "We found the light in the night. They have to come home."

Henry wants to believe him. He sees Steeplechase

smolder, but the sky is clear and the Wonder Wheel stands firm:

W E... W E

On the boardwalk, everyone is talking nonsense, including Mingus Lamont, who is singing about a tuna in his pocket. A half-dozen policemen from Flushing are questioning the Funny Face punks, whose answers evoke hilarious laughter. Angelica and Rita are counting the stars that have so long been invisible. Myrtle Crespi, smelling of fried wires and smoke, skips up and hugs Henry and Buff both. "Wasn't it beautiful?" she asks. "Most beautiful thing I ever saw..."

Doc Couney, his hair on end from his open-air car-ride from Flushing, pulls Buff into an unusually eager embrace.

"What did you see Doc?" asks the boy when the old man releases him.

"Vell. I saw a dove, of course."

He pivots and points beyond the starry remnants of the new moon's birth to yet another strange sight in the sky. Clearing the far edge of the Wonder Wheel is a small cloud shaped like a mushroom and sporting a dangling pair of legs.

For the last time that night, Buff runs.

Paloma lands with a bump but she is already talking a mile a minute when Buff reaches her.

"It's so simple. Of course that's where they would go. I mean you wanna escape – you go far, far away. I mean it's plain as day…good golly, Buff. Did you see it? Did ya?"

Buff hurries to help his friend out of the parachute's harness. He understands. Paloma, from her exceptional vantage point has seen what no one else saw.

"There was a ring around Luna," she explains when she is free of the contraption that has carried her home. "I thought for a minute I was, you know, hallelujahnating. But then there was an arrow, like a bolt of lightning, shot from out there in the ocean, and BOOM – pointed the way. C'mon!"

They are already down the stairs and dodging through the fire engines on Surf Avenue when Buff cries, "Where are we going!?"

"Where Luna parks her ship, of course."

July 5, 1939
New Moon

It is quiet inside the midnight park when the Mermother emerges from the Trip to the Moon. She appears like a mirage passing through the shadow of the dark ride. But when she stamps her foot on Luna's ground, both are solid. She is dressed in the fitted green suit that Buff has already seen, but she wears her crown, from which she plucks another pearl. She bends and flicks the pearl like a shooter marble. As it travels across the ground, the hours of night roll with it. The pearl comes to a stop at the foot of the two Incubator Babies before her.

"You have delivered the new moon," she says with a smile.

She raises her chin slightly and Buff and Paloma follow her gaze. The sky over the Rockaways is rosy.

When they turn back, the Mermother is gone. In her place are two children: a girl with blonde braids and a boy with a crooked green bow tie. Oscar and Mary Lou. They blink at the lucid dawn. They sniff the air, which is sharp and clean. They turn and beckon to the door of the dark ride.

Buff squeezes Paloma's hand as the others step out into the morning – five, ten, a dozen, two dozen. Bare-kneed, clean-scrubbed, a skip in their step and a giggle on their lips, the children are singing a song both Buff and Paloma recognize.

Ashes, ashes…We all come home.

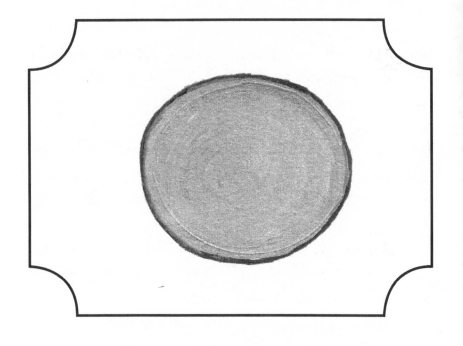

Epilogue
Full Moon
September 1, 1940

A year and some months have passed since the strange events of the wee hours of July 5, 1939. Coney Island, with the help of a rebuilt Steeplechase Park under new management, has had a banner season. Inspector Ramsey, promoted shortly after the bust on the pier, made it his first order of duty to triple the number of police on beat at Coney Island; not a single child has gone missing for longer than twenty-five minutes at the beach this summer.

Buff is closing his story-telling booth for the season and maybe, he's thinking, for good. He will be fifteen soon. He's more interested in biology than tall tales, and Doc has signed him up as a volunteer at Brooklyn Hospital—the first hospital to purchase an infant incubator for its baby ward.

Anyway, Buff has told his best stories more times than he can count.

Except for the story of the moon egg. He doesn't tell that story, because he knows it still has not ended. He sleeps soundly at night, forgetting his dreams by morning. But on nights when the moonlight is playful, the boy senses a message— a reminder that there are still battles ahead for Coney Island and strange champions, too. A reminder that the future is uncertain.

Coney Island is closing for the season, but the World's Fair is closing forever. Many New Yorkers, including some from Coney Island, wept when they said goodbye to the Fair. Because the World of Tomorrow had, in fact, proved to be the nail in the coffin. Not for Coney Island, but for that decade of lost dreams and broken lives that went down in history as the Great Depression. The 1939 World's Fair was a source of great inspiration for New York and for the nation. But in the fall of 1940, there are fresh concerns.

When the crew comes to raze the Perisphere, it is given instructions: not a shard of steel is to be wasted. That's because the World is at War. Germany has sent its army into Poland and will not stop there. All of Europe is in danger.

America is limited in her powers of salvation. Like the Mermother, there is not much she can do until she is willing to come out of (or in this case, to cross) the water. Plenty of voices are calling for the country to enter the fight. Dr. Martin Couney is among the loudest, though he limits his urgent exhortations to letters to Congress, knowing that his heavy accent confuses people about the nature of his loyalty. Handsome Henry has refused to wait. He has already sailed for Europe. He has vowed to protect the mothers and children being hunted by the Chancellor or to die trying.

At home, Coney Island is still at war with the Commissioner. He is stronger than ever, and he is planning attacks with surveyors and demolition machines. But he cannot win every skirmish. When the committee asks him what is to be done with the Parachute Jump, he thinks of the grey-eyed boy and his brave friend who flew from the Jump, and he softens.

"Send it to Coney Island," he says.

And so Coney gets a new ride. A crew of handsome young men is trained to run the Jump, which quickly replaces the Pavilion of Fun as the most popular attraction on Coney Island. There is a girl on the squad too. She's the only girl—past, present or future—who will ever work the Parachute Jump, and she commands a great deal of respect. She is, of course, Paloma.

It's Paloma's day off and she's helping Buff clear out his booth. She pulls a box from under the counter and rummages inside. There's a stack of curled up comic books and a dusty salt-stained rucksack. She hands the sack to Buff.

"Seems awful small to have held what it did," he says.

The two friends don't talk about the night when they helped find more than two dozen lost kids and drive a heavy shroud of despair from their home. It's not an easy thing to talk about when you're nearly fifteen and less willing to speak of magic and mermaids and miracles. Instead, they speak in code. They speak of things that happened in "the waning years," meaning before that night of adventure, and of things "today" -- things that they recognize, without saying so, as being possible only because of the bravery they shared and the Ring Around Luna they helped draw. These things they sometimes call "lunatic."

The clock tower chimes six and Paloma jumps up.

"Gotta go Buff, my ma's made dinner and I promised to bring a pie." Paloma's mother has made some changes this year too. She quit her job at the dancehall, signed up for training in a nearby workshop painting carousel horses, and moved into a tidy cottage about a half a mile from the Bowery. She's home every night, which Paloma mostly likes. That will change in a year or two, when Paloma starts wishing her ma didn't always ask where she was off to now?

She's halfway out the door when she turns.

"Buff?"

He looks up from the mildewed rucksack.

"Did you really know that it was the moon?"

He is surprised. Since she has never asked, he has never needed to answer.

"I don't know," he says now. "Do you really think the woman who brought them back vanished into the sea? Do you really believe that the police came to Coney Island in its hour of need just to arrest Paloma Bright?"

Paloma smiles a smug smile. "Coney has always been a fine home for whattayacallems – narcissists," she says. "Do you want to come over for dinner?"

Buff shakes his head. "Doc's expecting me. He's got a cold and I promised to bring him hot dogs. He says wieners are even better than penicillin."

Paloma waves goodbye and is gone.

Buff sits alone in the dust rays of early evening, absentmindedly spinning the last of his hard-earned dimes across the counter. Finally, he stands and, taking the rucksack with him, leaves his stall. He walks unhurriedly through Luna Park, greeting the carnies and the gamers and the vendors as he passes.

Surf Avenue is crowded with families headed for the subway and couples headed for the music halls. The line in front of the Loews Theater winds all the way down the block. Buff stops at Nathan's and buys four hot dogs.

He's decided to follow the boardwalk home, so he tugs off his shoes to feel the last warmth of summer on the planks. Just past the Parachute Jump, Buff jumps down onto the sand. Behind him a brand new Funny Face wiggles its eyes back and forth, looking for seaside mischief. On the horizon a full moon tries to make itself seen against a golden sunset, patiently waiting for nightfall.

The sea is quiet – the water near the buoy-bell at the end of the Dreamland Pier is still. Buff has not seen the

Mermother since the night the egg hatched; He is, as always, motherless. He tells himself others need her more. He tells himself that her absence is a sign that, for all the uncertainty the world faces as the summer of 1940 draws to a close, Coney Island is in a moment of security. He tells himself he needs no proof that she exists or even that, if Coney Island should need her again, she will return. But he sometimes wonders…

The wet sand changes color under Buff's feet as the surf washes in and out. It reminds him of the subtle changes that drifted across the surface of the pearl during that strange fortnight last summer. He thinks about the mysteries held in the eerie, smooth container – about the secrets that he would never understand, even the one that he had, in fact, cracked.

At the edge of the water, the hermit crabs leave holes in the sand as they burrow deeper against the tide. The holes make a pattern, like a perforated message. Buff steps further out into the waves to read what it says:

Well done, he reads, *well done.*

And then the message is gone.

ELIZABETH KIEM is a reader and a writer. In the summer of 2007 she rode her bicycle down to Coney Island every day, but now she lives in London, and that's too far a ride.

MILLICENT HODSON is a choreographic detective who recreates lost ballets. That's why her Lunatics always appear to be dancing. She, too, lives in London, just up the street from Elizabeth.

Made in the USA
Columbia, SC
04 September 2017